THE SHADOWS OF SEVILLE

David Canford

To the wonderful women in my life: Mary, Megan, Toria, and Millie

CHAPTER 1

It was a cruel beauty which enveloped him in the dappled sunlight, a beauty which teased with promise, a promise which wouldn't be kept. Yet the pink blossom of the almond trees, like a long line of nature's bridesmaids, brought the trace of a smile to Ramon's face while he trudged home amongst them. It was something delightful in a life that lacked delight.

When the almonds finally came, Ramon wouldn't get to savour them. Don Pedro Castillo Morales had warned his workers that if anybody dared to take some, the culprit would be dismissed and his relatives would suffer the same fate.

"Betray me and you betray your family too." The man was uncompromising, as always.

It was the same with the olives. Don Pedro had even forbidden picking up windfalls that would rot on the ground.

He hated the new government. Communists, Don Pedro called them, although only a handful of seats in the Cortes, the Spanish parliament, had been won by the Communist Party. He resented that the government was passing laws to reduce working hours, which ran from dawn to dusk, and laws to increase wages so low they condemned the peasants of Spain to dire poverty and an existence often on the verge of starvation.

"Blame those Reds in Madrid! All was fine until they interfered." Addressing his labourers, Don Pedro had shaken his fist in anger as if a man possessed. "And don't come to me complaining about what you think you should be paid or asking for shorter working hours. If you don't like my terms, you can go elsewhere. I can bring in workers from Portugal, they'd be glad to have your jobs, or maybe I'll just stop cultivation altogether. I will not be dictated to, by you or anyone else."

The workers kept their heads bowed, acting as if they were mute. Nobody challenged him, they couldn't afford to lose their employment.

Dirt under his fingernails and feet the colour of the ochre earth he toiled upon, Ramon walked as if lead weights were tied to his ankles. Twelve hours of work, six days a week, exhausted even a young man like him. Next week would be no different, no different to the lives of millions in this land of sunshine and bounty, a bounty owned and controlled by a select few.

The Catholic Church told the labourers they would be rewarded in heaven if they kept to a narrow path of hard work, obedience, and virtue. That they might live a life of suffering here on earth was deemed to be of no consequence given the promise of heaven which awaited those who adhered to the scriptures.

Ramon's calf muscles protested while he climbed the steep path to his village perched on a rocky outcrop overlooking hectares of farmland. Farmland which all belonged to one family.

At this time of year there was greenery and soon wildflowers would appear, creating a profusion of colour like an Impressionist's painting. It would look idyllic to those from afar who might pass through Andalusia's countryside and see only nature's magnificence, unaware of the circumstances in which the vast majority of the locals lived. The burned brown of summer that reflected the harshness of existence in this land was still months away.

In the distance stood the grand hacienda of Don Pedro, a powerful statement of his wealth. The large, white building with terracotta roof tiles faced south. There were no windows at the rear, its back turned on the village where his workers lived. Vines, which would produce grapes for the sherry so loved by the British, ran in neat rows. The whinnying of the family's fine thoroughbreds pierced the evening stillness while vultures circled on thermals high above, searching for something dead or dying. For most in rural Spain, the line between life and death was a brittle one.

Tomorrow was Sunday and there would be some time to relax. Ramon's mother would insist they attend Mass. And now there was added pressure, talk that the priest had taken to sending a note to Don Pedro after a service of those who'd failed to attend. The two men would assume that those who didn't were suspect, almost certainly leftists and not true patriots. Men who absented themselves would risk being fired.

Ramon pushed open the wooden door to the family home, a door rotten with woodworm and whose planks no longer hung flush together, the gaps growing wider each year. The small house was part of a long line of single-storey, lime-washed buildings. Their external cheery, white brightness was deceptive. Inside the floor was earthen and the light gloomy, illuminated by only a small fire above which hung their one cooking pot. His mother was bent before it, stirring.

Only forty, a hard life had given her the appearance of a much greater age. Her hair was already grey. When she smiled these days, which was rarely, it was with a deliberately closed mouth to hide her missing teeth. Teeth which she had insisted her son help her yank out with the aid of string to end the pain they were causing. Her dress was black and that colour would be her only option for the rest of her days now she was a widow.

In a corner, Ramon's sister, Carmelita, was crouched on the floor, her head bowed as if in prayer. Although only sixteen, whenever she went out she stooped like an old woman and looked down at the ground. It was her method of trying to conceal her disfigurement and avoid the unwelcome stares, and eyes which often reflected horror, sometimes disgust, should she raise her head.

Carmelita spoke only if she had to. She hated the nasal sound she made, and her difficulty with pronunciation embarrassed her. A large part of her upper lip was missing. Instead, a gap in her flesh reached her nose. Born with a cleft lip, Carmelita was ashamed of how she looked and how she sounded.

Ramon wanted nothing more than to earn enough to pay for an operation for his sister. People saw only her mouth which they considered ugly and repulsive. They didn't notice her striking ebony eyes or the love and gentleness within her.

Ramon's heart ached that they didn't have the money needed for surgery. With his father gone and only one paltry wage coming in, the prospect of ever being able to save enough had receded yet further into the distant future.

When their meagre meal was over and the fire died, they would lie down and sleep, mother and sister on a bed close to collapse behind a rough wooden partition, and Ramon on straw upon the floor on the other side. Light from candles was a luxury and saved for Saints' days.

If there was a moon large enough to banish total darkness, Ramon and his mother would sit outside and chat with neighbours while the outline of skinny cats brushed past them and the brays of donkeys travelled in from the surrounding countryside. Their life was little more than medieval.

Come morning, Ramon reluctantly accompanied his mother and sister towards the solitary tolling bell which irritated him rather than uplifted him. Inside the church was a wealth he could only dream of, golden effigies of the Virgin Mary and of Jesus on the cross, and large golden candlesticks on the altar.

As always, the Castillo family were seated in the front pew resplendent in fine clothes, doubtless purchased in Paris which they were said to visit frequently. Don Pedro turned his head occasionally, checking on who had come and twisting his lips in a manner that caused his thin moustache, curled at both ends, to undulate like a seesaw.

To his left was his wife, an elaborate black lace mantilla on her head to demonstrate her piety. On his other side sat Francisco, their son and heir. Not much older than Ramon, he was very much his father's son both in temperament and outlook. A young man who treated Ramon and the other labourers with the same contempt his father did.

The priest, an overweight yet severe and joyless man, ascended into the pulpit. A man who lived in comfort in the largest house in the village which Carmelita cleaned. Paid so little for her work, it could be said she, rather than the priest, was performing an act of charity. There her nostrils would be taunted by the mouth watering smell of goat stews and fine hams coming from the kitchen where a cook would prepare the priest's meals. Meals of a type most of his flock could only imagine.

The priest's sermon was similar to last week's and the week before that. "Do not succumb to the temptations of Satan, personified today in our godless government in Madrid. A cabal that pursues a policy of ending the Church's control of education. They want to secularise our children and deny them the benefit of a Christian upbringing. A government that rejects the holy sacrament of marriage, and says a Church wedding is no longer sufficient and requires a civil ceremony, a government that disregards God's sacred word and permits the sin of divorce. Pray, yes pray I tell you with all your might for this anti-Christ of a government to be overthrown." The man's voice had risen to fever pitch, his knuckles whitening as he gripped the pulpit tightly in a fervour of righteousness. "The hour fast approaches when all God fearing Christians must rise up, rise up in the name of Christ and reclaim this blessed land for our Lord. As Ferdinand and Isabella conquered and drove out the Moors, so must we conquer and drive out the atheists."

He came to an abrupt halt, surveying his impassive congregation with beady eyes while seeking to determine how many had already been corrupted, swayed by the promise of a better life if they supported the parties of the left.

Ramon observed the confusion in his mother's eyes, conflicted by an inculcation since birth that the Church was infallible. Ramon, on the other hand, had no doubt the old order was wrong and inhumane, and that change was needed, fairness and justice for all, not just the privileged few.

"And now," commanded the priest in obsequious conclusion, "let us pray for Don Pedro Castillo Morales and his family, without whose generosity we would all be unemployed and hungry."

CHAPTER 2

Later that day, the rhythmic sound of a horse's hooves on the cobbles pricked Ramon's curiosity. Opening the creaking door, he saw the rear of a wooden wagon, its intricate woodwork painted in a lurid green and red. It continued down the street towards the small square in front of the church. His intention to follow and investigate was diverted by his mother's call to come eat.

Ramon had forgotten about the visitors until evocative cries which seemed to echo across the centuries drew him and the rest of the villagers out of their homes and towards the square.

"Gitanos," announced one man with disdain, spitting on the ground for emphasis.

Already falling, the sun's rays shone like a stage light through the space in the church tower around the bell.

A man with a prominent scar across his cheek stood next to a younger one seated on the church steps, a guitar resting on his crossed legs. Both were swarthy and Bohemian in appearance. From behind the nearby wagon, emerged a young woman in red, her dress hugging her figure and flaring out in a cascade of ruffles nearer the ground. Her gait was fierce and proud. She walked onto a wooden board placed in front of her two companions. Her obsidian eyes were defiant and confident, and her black hair swept back in a chignon highlighted her prominent cheek bones.

Mesmerised, the villagers gawked in anticipatory silence. Slowly and gracefully she raised her arms above her head, her slender finger tips almost touching. She leaned backwards, arching her back like a viper preparing to lunge at its victim. The young man began playing the guitar and guttural, primeval cries came from the older man by his side.

The dancer's movements gradually quickened, the stamping of her feet echoing around the square like rapid gunfire. She took hold of the lower part of her dress moving it first one way, then another, twisting, twirling, going ever faster and faster, and now trance like as if she inhabited another reality.

Ramon swallowed hard, transfixed by her exotic beauty and overt sensuality. Never had he seen someone so exquisite, so intoxicating, so free of inhibition.

The older man clapped to the rhythm, urging her on, on to the climax of the dance. When it suddenly and unexpectedly ended the crowd called for more. Regally, the dancer assumed her starting position, preparing herself.

"Stop!" An angry shout rang out. "This is sacrilege.

How dare you perform here before God's house, and during Lent."

The priest had emerged from his home. Puce with fury, he harangued the audience. "Help me drive these devil worshippers out of here."

Bending down, he picked up a stone and threw it at the dancer. His aim was true and her head shot backwards on contact. When she raised her head, Ramon stared at her. Blood ran from her nose. She returned Ramon's stare, their eyes engaging for a moment.

"You bastard!" Enraged, Ramon ran at the priest. Others joined him. Sensing imminent defeat, the man turned and hurried to his door, bolting it the instant he was inside.

"Come out or we'll burn you out," yelled one of the men. "Your kind are no longer going to subjugate us with your threats and lies." A roar of agreement erupted. Encouraged by the support, the self-appointed spokesperson continued, "Leave this village and never come back. You have two minutes to collect your things."

The air became heavy with a loud quiet. The door opened slowly and with hesitation. The priest appeared, carrying nothing and avoiding eye contact. The crowd drew back to let him through. Reaching the nearest alley, he scurried away.

"A rat fleeing to safety. He'll be off to Don Pedro's. Who'll join me first thing tomorrow to occupy that tyrant's land and free ourselves from a life no better than slavery?" Several offered their support, including Ramon.

A calloused hand gripped his bare arm and pulled it. "Come, let's get back."

"In a minute." He scanned the square for the dancer but the wagon had gone.

"Now," insisted his mother.

"What on earth did you think you were doing? The priest is God's representative." Ramon's mother reprimanded him.

"No, he's Don Pedro's servant, not God's. Part of the hierarchy which oppresses us and keeps us in poverty. Open your eyes. How can it be right that Papa died because we couldn't afford a doctor while a few live in luxury and the rest of us barely survive?"

"Well, whatever the rights or wrongs of our situation, there'll be trouble now. You'll be a marked man, accused of being one of the ringleaders. There were those who didn't join in, taking note of those who did. They're probably in the pay of Don Pedro. You need to leave and go to Seville, a city you can easily disappear into."

"Leave? You mean run like a coward," protested Ramon. "And what about you and Carmelita?"

"We'll manage, and you can send us money when you find a job. We won't manage if they kill you. Your first duty is to your family. Carmelita will never get a husband, you know that. Remember how you swore to your father on his deathbed that you would take care of her, always. To honour that oath, you need to stay alive. Be the man you promised to be, Ramon. Go. Go tonight." His mother spoke with an unshakeable determination.

She tugged at the ring on the third finger of her left hand. The years had welded it to her flesh. After several twists and pulls, it finally came off leaving an indentation on her finger. "Here, take your grandmother's ring. You can sell it so you have some money to get settled."

The onyx ring set on a silver band, though tarnished with age, was his mother's most treasured possession.

"No, you must keep it. You might need to sell it to buy food for you and Carmelita."

"I insist. You'll more than repay us, I know you will. You are our pride and joy. Go with God."

For a moment she stood looking at her son, imprinting his features on her memory. That full, square face she so adored, tanned even at this time of year from toiling outside every day, his thick hair of deep chestnut and his olive green eyes. She placed her hands on his arms, and, on tiptoes, kissed his cheek, her eyes glistening with tears she was fighting to suppress. Opening the door, she gently but firmly pushed him out into the night.

CHAPTER 3

Beatriz ran her index finger down her nose and exhaled with relief. The stone thrown so accurately by the priest hadn't broken it. Her immediate concern when she jumped up into the wagon was that her nose would be forever changed, transformed into one which was crooked or squashed. Something which could have jeopardised her dancing career before it had really begun.

Her perfectly proportioned, unblemished face was her greatest attribute. It was all she possessed apart from her clothes. Eighteen years of age, she still had much to learn as a dancer but her striking looks would be a crucial ingredient in any future success.

Beatriz curled up on the bench which also served as a bed, but sleep wouldn't come. The wagon jolted and juddered on the uneven dirt track and thoughts of this evening repeated themselves. Yet she knew tonight could have been worse. Her kind were despised by most, distrusted and blamed for many things.

In the cities, they had their own areas where by force of numbers they were less vulnerable. Out here they stood out, people who were different, people who weren't regarded as really Spanish. Their very name, gitanos, a corruption of egiptanos, meaning Egyptians in Old Spanish, marked them out as foreigners by origin, people who had migrated from India via the Middle East. Centuries ago the Jews were expelled from Spain as were the Moors. Why not expel the gitanos also, many would ask.

Beatriz disliked their winter travels out to the country. The open space felt unsafe and filled her soul with emptiness. She loved to dance, it was already her passion, but arriving in each new place was a daunting experience, not knowing if they would be tolerated to perform or be chased out like lepers. Today it had been a stone, tomorrow it might be a bullet.

It was good practice, a chance to improve her art, and her brother his guitar playing, her father told her. A chance to earn a few pesetas too, though these days their takings were sparse.

Beatriz longed to be back home amongst familiarity, to dance for her own kind, not strangers whose mood could flip from approval to hostility in an instant.

Regardless of their reception, they never spent the night in a village where they performed. Her father and brother said it wasn't safe. Beatriz understood why. Her dancing could arouse men.

Men who might think they had the right to succumb to their feelings because her moves, they would tell themselves, showed she was a woman without virtue. Beatriz's father and brother each slept with a dagger by their side.

"Padre Alfonso is here to see you," announced the maid.

"At this hour of the evening," muttered Don Pedro, his irritation undisguised.

The priest entered the room, a fire and loathing in his eyes. He didn't bother with customary greetings. "I've been driven from my home by a Communist mob."

"Oh, my goodness," exclaimed Doña Maria, raising her hand to her mouth.

Don Pedro leapt up from his chair. "Where did they come from? Where are they now?"

"It was the villagers, many of whom were in church this morning, feigning obedience to God's word. A band of filthy gitanos arrived to perform their lascivious dancing, and when I demanded it end I was turned upon. And that is not all. As I departed, I heard them discussing how tomorrow they would invade your lands. It's happening elsewhere in the country, a complete breakdown of law and order."

Don Pedro stuck out his jaw. "Well, it won't happen here. Francisco and I will be waiting for them. I'll have a room made up for you tonight, Padre, and by tomorrow evening you'll be back in your home, of that you can rest assured."

Armed with sticks and a few old rifles which would most probably misfire, men from the village made their way down the track. The dim, crepuscular light was strengthening under a sky streaked with vermilion and purple. Soon the sun would breach the horizon. For once, the men appreciated the beauty of dawn and ignored the early morning chill. Today would be like no other, not another day of drudgery and backbreaking work for somebody else. After a lifetime of subservience, today was the day it would end, the day when they would take control of their destiny and become men instead of mice.

Rounding a bend they came to an abrupt halt. Five men on horseback blocked their way.

"What do you think you're doing?" demanded Don Pedro from his elevated position.

"We're taking over," replied one of the villagers. "We don't want violence, and there'll be none if you co-operate."

"Co-operate," repeated Don Pedro with a derisory sneer. "I don't co-operate with robbers and thieves. This land is my land, and mine alone. This isn't Russia, it is Spain. Drop your weapons and get to work before I dismiss all of you."

The two groups eyeballed each other, tension building. Without warning, Don Pedro removed his pistol from its holster and fired several shots in rapid succession. Three men fell to the ground, writhing in agony. Pre-empting possible retaliation, the other horsemen aimed their guns at the protesters.

Sensing victory from the workers' expressions of surprise and indecision, Don Pedro drove home his advantage. "Go back to the hovels you climbed out of. My farm is closed, and you are no longer employed. And don't get any ideas, the Civil Guard has been informed and will be here soon to arrest any man remaining."

With an arrogant confidence, he pulled on the reins, turning his stallion sharply. The men he'd shot in the legs would struggle to ever work again, and the rest had been taught a lesson. He had done enough. Within days, they'd be forced to return, begging for work, and he would agree to take them back. For lower pay than before.

"Don't ever compromise," he instructed his son while they trotted home. "If you show even a hint of weakness, you'll be finished. It's you or them, it's that simple. Never forget that."

CHAPTER 4

Ramon walked all night to keep warm. When the sun rose, he lay down near the roadside and slept. His eyelids flickered and he raised his arm to shield his eyes from the midday sun. Ramon got up but stumbled, his rope sandals were disintegrating. He tossed them aside and continued barefoot, seeking to avoid the sharp stones that somehow always managed to catch him out and caused him to jump in painful surprise whenever he stood on one.

It was late afternoon when he saw her in the distance. He had never seen anything like her before. Seville, the largest city in Andalusia. All his life his horizons had been limited, small and unexciting. Ramon's heart quickened, energised by the possibility of a future which could be different, a life that wouldn't be already predetermined, and a life which needn't be wasted as a virtual serf.

His awe and wonder only increased when he drew closer. Several motor vehicles had already passed him. In his village, the only car was the one owned by Don Pedro. A screech of metal against metal made him start and a tram rattled past.

It was as though Ramon had walked into a different country. On the boulevard, more people than he'd ever seen ambled along. A few were in threadbare clothing, looking as destitute as him, yet many were dressed in a finery to rival Don Pedro and his wife.

Evening was already ushering out another day and Ramon needed a place to sleep. He crossed the wide avenue to a park which might offer a night he could spend unnoticed. Among a lush growth of palm trees and shrubs, he found a secluded spot. Tired from his long walk, sleep came despite the complaints of his empty stomach. Hunger was something he was accustomed to, something millions of Spaniards suffered from most of the time.

When morning woke him with a cold damp lick of dew, Ramon left his den. Following a pathway, he reached a large open space. He gaped while his eyes drank in the scale of the building before him. Ramon had happened upon a huge, two-storey semi-circular structure of sun-kissed brown. Tall, domed towers, layered like wedding cakes, stood at either end of the curved building, and a moat of opaque teal encased the large open space in front of it. He moved closer, crossing a small bridge over the moat and placed his hand on the colourful blue, white, and yellow tiling on one of the attractive lamp stands while he took time to absorb this magnificent sight.

The first floor was arcaded and below was yet more colourful tile work representing scenes from every province in Spain. It was a place of a grandeur and beauty the likes of which he had never seen before. Ramon concluded this must be La Plaza de España, constructed only a few years earlier for the Ibero-American fair of 1929. An exposition intended to put Seville back on the map after so many years of decline. The United States and the countries of South America had also participated, creating their own pavilions. Like others in his village, Ramon had heard of the event but nobody was able to afford a bus ride to Seville to see it.

Ramon continued with a spring in his step. Walking past the orange trees in bloom that lined the surrounding streets, he breathed in their sweet and creamy fragrance, which infused him with hope. Maybe he would indeed find a better future in this city of enchantment.

All day long he stopped at bars, restaurants, and workshops. None of them had any vacancies. His walk slowed and his shoulders sagged, his balloon of exhilaration deflated. Even the spectacular architecture he was passing failed to revive him. Instead, the thought of food hijacked all his attention.

Ramon realised he had no choice. He entered a shop with bars at the windows behind which lay the most precious possessions of those who had gone before him, forced to part with things which were so much more than what others saw in them. Items that were irreplaceable, a treasured gift from a loved one or an heirloom passed down through the generations, each carrying a unique and personal story.

The owner's greeting was a grunt and his wily face implacable, hardened from years of hearing others' pleas for more.

"How much?" asked Ramon, producing from his trouser pocket the ring his mother had given him.

The man examined it only briefly. "Ten pesetas."

"Ten? It's got to be worth much more than that."

"Fifteen. That's my final offer. I'm running a business, not a charity."

"A hundred."

The man snorted with laughter and thrust the ring back at Ramon. "Leave, you're wasting my time."

Ramon was forced to accept the inevitable. "All right, I'll take fifteen."

"You have a month to reclaim it for thirty or it goes in the window and might be sold before you can buy it back."

Ramon went straight to the nearest bar to eat and then retreated back to the park where he'd spent the previous night. Despite sheltering under a tree, heavy rain drenched him.

Come morning the rain had ceased but dawn revealed a sky of tombstone grey matching Ramon's mood. He fretted he would run out of money and could be forced to beg like those he'd seen outside the cathedral, their heads down in shame and hands out, hoping somebody might throw them a few centimos. Worse was the sapping fear he would have nothing to send his mother and sister. Constant rejection was grinding him down and failure becoming a self-fulfilling prophecy.

When he entered a cafe late that morning, he swooned at the rich aroma of fresh coffee and something else he didn't recognise but which smelled as comforting as a mother's hug. The establishment was narrow and crowded, servers on one side of a long counter and customers on the other, and a patterned blue-tiled wall and glass fronted cupboards stocked with bottles behind them. In between clients and servers sat the source of what Ramon had been unable to identify, although it had already seduced his nose. Finger-like pieces of fried dough occupied plates next to cups of dark liquid chocolate into which the lucky customers were dipping them before quickly popping them into their mouths to avoid a drip of chocolate falling on their clothes.

"Churros?" asked a portly man behind the counter, noticing the look of intense desire on Ramon's face.

"No. I came to enquire if you might need help." So low were his expectations Ramon wasn't expecting the answer he received.

"In fact, I do. We were broken into last night.

The city is becoming unsafe. It's too bad General Sanjurjo's coup failed. He would have given us back the law and order this country so desperately needs." Ramon nodded, he knew he mustn't give the man cause to think he was a supporter of the government in Madrid or he would stand no chance of being employed. An attempted coup in 1932 failed everywhere except Seville where Sanjurjo, who had the appearance of a mafia boss, had taken control for twenty-four hours. "I want someone to sleep here to protect my business and to run errands for me during the day. Go sit at one of the tables in the back and I'll join you."

Ramon fought to focus and give the correct replies to the questions the proprietor asked of him, but the churros and cup of chocolate the man brought for Ramon threatened to distract him. Never had he tasted anything so incredible. The bitter sweetness of the chocolate mixed with the salty and oily aromas of the crunchy churro were a heavenly combination. Ramon ate only one. He needed to concentrate on getting this job, not momentary pleasure, even if this was the most incredible thing he'd ever eaten.

"I came in from the country. Jobs out there are in short supply, and I need to support my mother and sister so they don't go hungry. I'm used to hard work. Please, Señor, give me a chance, I promise not to disappoint you."

The man eyed him quizzically. "Are you a leftist?"

"No," lied Ramon. "They're causing trouble,

intimidating those of us who refuse to rebel, and annoying the bosses who then stop cultivating their land, resulting in the rest of us going without anything to eat."

"Hmm. Well, you look like a donkey dragged you in from the fields, but I wouldn't want your family to starve. I'll give you a trial." Ramon was too overwhelmed to speak, blinking back tears of relief. "Gonzalez is my name. Finish your churros and I'll be back with some money so you can buy appropriate clothing. You can pay me back from your wages."

Ramon grinned for the rest of the day. Once more he noticed the beauty of the city, smelled its sensual promise.

Ramon discovered that not only could he dine on churros late every night when the place shut but that the establishment also served meals which were a perk of the job for those working there. Ramon had never eaten like this. Meat every day, something which had been an extremely rare treat at home and used to consist of little more than gristle and fat. While he chewed pork so tender it almost melted in his mouth, Ramon was pricked with pangs of guilt, thinking of the pitiful rations Carmelita and his mother would be living on.

As soon as he could, Ramon began sending them money and spent the absolute minimum on himself. The job wasn't well paid but he didn't have the cost of buying food or renting a room which more than made up for his low wages.

Alone each night, he lined up four straight-backed dining chairs and lay down on them. He'd never slept in a proper bed so the hard wood didn't bother him.

Before opening time, he washed himself using the sink in the customer bathroom. Ramon liked the new man he saw looking back at him in the mirror; his hair neatly combed and greased, a white shirt and black trousers. The most wonderful thing of all were his polished black shoes, the first pair of shoes Ramon had ever owned.

His family would be so proud if they could see him, but that didn't seem to be something which would happen soon. His mother had written a reply to the letter he'd sent her, or rather she'd gone to a neighbour who had written the letter for her, to tell him there had been violence and not to return to the village.

CHAPTER 5

Izil sat down on a rock. It was uneven and cold but his legs ached from many hours of standing. A drop of snot formed on the end of his nose and he pulled up the hood of his brown woollen djellaba to give protection from the biting wind. Their ribs clearly visible, the family's goats had their heads down, seeking green shoots in this lunar-like landscape.

Far below, the Mediterranean sparkled as if a polished jewel, and the whitewashed buildings of Tetouan near the coast were almost blinding in their brightness. Yet up in the Rif mountains of Northern Morocco spring was capricious. Overnight, snow had fallen. Eking out an existence on these vertiginous slopes wasn't easy, particularly during the long winter months.

Izil rehearsed his speech, nervous at what his father's reaction would be. But he knew he must do this, do something to improve their dire situation. Sometimes to survive it was necessary to make a bargain with the devil.

Izil was an Amazigh, a people who collectively

called themselves Imazighen, meaning free people. Europeans referred to them by the name the Romans used, Berbers.

The young man's hair was short but thick with tight black curls, his nose large but not unattractive. A thin beard covered his lower chin and cheeks and his eyes conveyed a quiet dignity.

Getting up, Izil shouted at the goats and shooed them with his stick towards a flat-roofed stone house grimly clinging to the mountainside. Two children in scruffy clothes ran around in the patchy snow. To them it was a delight to be enjoyed, not something which added to the daily struggle to survive.

Leaving the animals and their earthy smell on the lower floor, Izil climbed the ladder to the living quarters where his mother and father were seated on a rug. His father would spend the day there until they carried him to bed, his legs useless since he had been caught in a rockslide. The man wore a turban and the woman a scarf on her head, both by tradition and to give some warmth. The tentacles of the wind, which rarely ceased to blow up here in the mountains, found their way in through every gap in the stonework.

"I need to talk to you," began Izil. "I'm signing up."

"Signing up?"

"With the Regulares, the Africanista corps."

"Joining our oppressors!" exclaimed his father. "Surely you haven't forgotten all that I've told you. About how they brutalised our people after we rose up in our fight for freedom when you were but a young child. The Spanish soldiers smiled while they posed for photographs holding the decapitated heads of our men. They dropped toxic gas bombs upon us, killing our women and children."

"I know, father. I won't forget who I am, never. But how else do you suggest I take care of this family? Many of our young men have already signed up. They didn't do it for love of the infidel but to give their families the life they deserve. I will earn good money and send it home to you. You'll be able to have the treatment you need, and mother won't have to lie awake at night worrying about how she's going to feed everyone. We only have two goats left and both of them are old."

His father's stare was dogmatic. "I'd rather starve."

"My mind is made up," replied Izil, unwilling to back down.

"If you go, don't come back."

"I have to do this, for you, for mother, for my little brother and sister. Please try to understand."

His father closed his eyes and shook his head. His mother's eyes brimmed with tears, unwilling to intervene and contradict her husband.

Determined, Izil climbed down the ladder. His stomach was churning from the confrontation, his father's reaction was as he feared it would be. Obeying his father's word would have been so much easier, easier until the family had no food left. This was the hardest thing he'd ever had to do but he had no choice. The luxury of choice was reserved for those with money.

Outside, his siblings ran over to him.

"Where are you off to?" asked Idir, his brother.

"I'm going away for a while to earn some money."

"Don't go," cried Tafrara, his sister, flinging her arms about his waist and laying her head against his body.

Izil hugged her back, battling the urge to stay. "I'll be home before you know it."

Farther down the track, he turned. They were still standing there, watching and waving. Izil quickened his pace.

Before long clouds obscured the mountain tops and fluffy white flakes began swirling around him, whispering temptation, temptation to rest. He resisted, in a couple of hours it would be dark and their softness would turn to ice. He needed to be at a much lower altitude if he wasn't to freeze to death.

Several times he stumbled on the scree. Dislodged rocks and stones crashed into others and sent more tumbling down the mountainside in an eerie cacophony as he fought for a firm foothold. Even after nightfall, when he risked inadvertently stepping off an edge into a void, Izil kept going. He was still too high.

Finally, snow no longer lit his way and the windchill lessened. Judging he'd descended far enough to survive the night, he got down on his haunches and huddled in his djellaba, exhausted from his journey and from defying his father.

Woken by the first rays of morning sun rising above the mountain peaks, Izil could see Tetouan, the capital of Spanish Morocco. Half a day's walk away were the barracks where he would begin a new life, one which would complete his exile from all he'd ever known.

CHAPTER 6

No longer having to worry about how he was going to survive, Ramon wandered the streets of Seville on his day off, endlessly fascinated by all he saw. Never had he conceived that a place so incredible could exist.

The cathedral, Catedral de Santa Maria de la Sede, sat like a queen bee in the centre, the largest Gothic cathedral in the world. Next to it, La Giralda, the imposing bell tower, thrusted skywards. Bathed in early morning light, their sand-coloured stone was particularly arresting.

The cathedral's interior made Ramon feel insignificant, lost in a soaring space of columns and vaults. The golden screen behind the main altar was larger than the entire front of the church in his village. Yet despite its glory, Ramon considered it wrong that so much wealth and power should be concentrated in an organisation that claimed to represent Jesus, a man who had preached giving everything away to help the poor, and when so many in Spain struggled to get by on so little.

Come Semana Santa, which ran from Palm Sunday to Easter Sunday, the city became hypnotised by a spectacle of religious devotion. Ramon joined the throngs cramming the streets to watch. Religious statues from churches across the city brought outside for the occasion were paraded on palos, or floats, telling the story of the Crucifixion and Resurrection, a tradition dating back four centuries. Weighing over a ton, the floats were born upon the necks and shoulders of costaleros, the men hidden by brocade which reached down to the ground to give the impression the floats were moving of their own volition. The costaleros were said to welcome the pain of carrying their heavy load because of the suffering Christ had endured.

Alongside walked nazarenos, appearing somewhat sinister in their long cloaks and stiffened conical hats with face coverings containing a small opening for each eye. Some were all in white, some wore red velvet hoods, others were dressed in purple or black. Several carried full size crosses and wore chains around their feet which dragged behind them. Contrary to the the Ku Klux Klan impression given, they were penitents. The hoods worn to show that everyone was equal in the eyes of God and that sinners could repent in anonymity. As dusk fell, a hush descended upon the crowd while a palo passed by on which lay a statue of the body of Jesus taken down from the cross, dressed only in a loincloth and a crown of thorns, and watched over by those who had loved him.

Beneath them was a bed of purple irises, and next to Jesus a single red rose to signify his blood.

An emotive but abrasive voice of gravel shattered the respectful silence. In unison the people turned towards the source, sung a cappella by a man on a balcony, his arms thrust out in passion. The raw intensity gripped Ramon, reminding him of the cries of the voice when flamenco had come to his village. He immediately thought of the dancer as he had many times already, wondering where she was and if she might be here, close by but unseen. She'd lit a flame in his heart which still burned.

Born aloft, there followed a float covered by a canopy supported by slender columns of silver. Behind large, thick candles was an effigy of the Virgin Mary, la Estrella (star), in a dress and headdress of white and gold. An elaborate, many pronged golden circular star was positioned above her head. Solitary glass tears on her rouged cheeks evoked the grief and empathy she was said to have for the troubles of believers. Floral showers of petals were thrown down at her from open windows and balconies, and the smell of incense was strong in the night air.

The processions would wind their way to the cathedral and then return to the individual churches from which they had come. Some would take more than ten hours to complete their journey.

Ramon couldn't help but be impressed by the scale of it all. If he needed reminding how deeply the old conservative and hierarchical order had rooted itself in Spanish society and what a monumental challenge bringing change would be, Semana Santa provided abundant proof.

Only a couple of weeks afterwards, Seville threw off her religious solemnity to party. The Feria d'Abril was a celebration like no other.

Once again, Ramon was astounded by the vibrancy of life here; the colour, the excitement, the joy. Women of all classes paraded in flamenco dresses in bright and bold, many with polka dots. The wealthy women made the journey in open carriages, pulled by handsome horses their manes braided with flowers. Others walked or made their way side saddle behind a vaquero, a cowboy, wearing his wide brimmed hat and short black jacket and trousers protected by leather chaps.

A warm breeze wafted the perfume of the señoritas towards Ramon. Laughter, spontaneous dancing, and copious amounts of sherry created a hedonism of damn tomorrow and live for today. Sevillanos prayed hard and played harder. He loved his new life, a life without fear, a life of freedom.

Ramon saw her, her back to him, that same red dress, the same perfect posture. His pulse accelerated.

"Hola!"

She turned her head and his hopes were dashed. He was mistaken, she wasn't the flamenco dancer who had come to his village. He sloped off, dispirited.

"You should be smiling, come dance with me," exclaimed a woman in a yellow flamenco dress and with large silver hoop earrings dangling from her ears.

"I don't know how."

"That doesn't matter, most of those here can't dance either."

She grabbed his hand and they melted into the crowd, all of whom were too absorbed with their own moves to notice anyone else. Nonetheless, Ramon felt ridiculous stamping his feet and moving his arms in an amateurish fashion even if his partner didn't seem to care.

"It's about enjoyment and passion," she shouted above the drumming of feet. After a short while, sensing his discomfort, she relented. "I'll put you out of your suffering, let's go get a drink."

"Erm-"

She pulled him by the hand once more, hers sweaty but smooth, a pull which wouldn't accept refusal. "I know, you're a poor young man. No need to worry, I'm rich."

Mariela was probably about his mother's age, but with a different life the passing of time had been considerably more forgiving, helped in part by a generous application of mascara and lipstick. Her scent was reminiscent of the orange blossom which had greeted his arrival in the city.

A shared jar of sangria loosened their tongues and chased away inhibition. Waking in silky sheets, a sensation Ramon had never experienced, he panicked. Ramon didn't know for how long it had been dark. Outside, passing revellers clapped out a flamenco beat but that brought him no comfort, Seville never slept during the Feria. Leaping out of bed, he dressed quickly.

Mariela stirred in the shadows cast by the moon, stretching her arms languidly above her head. "Where are you going? Come back to bed."

"I have to get to work."

"When will I see you again?"

"I don't know."

Ramon saw her a week later, seated on a stool in the cafe where he worked, a coffee and a plate of untouched churros on the counter top.

"I enjoy the smell but I don't eat them. It wouldn't be good for my figure." She took a sip of her coffee never once taking her piercing hazel eyes off him. "Why don't you come round later?"

Before Ramon could answer, she got up and left.

Succumbing to his instincts, Ramon arrived at her apartment early that evening. Their encounter was febrile and wordless. Afterwards, while Mariela lay in the crook of his arm, she surprised him.

"Señor Gonzalez is a good friend of mine. I asked him why your talents are being wasted. I think you can expect a promotion, and then you won't have to sleep there any longer."

"But I don't mind, it allows me to save more money

to help my family."

Mariela moved the bright red nail of a finger slowly across his bare chest and fixed him with a mischievous look. "You won't have to worry about that. I have an apartment in Triana that I'm not renting out at the moment. You can have it, for free."

As he wandered back to the bar, Ramon wondered if he should have felt conflicted. He was as good as selling himself for sex. This was his first affair, an initiation. A love for Mariela would never blossom. He was using her. Yet she was an adult, and was she not also using him? A plaything to distract herself from the emptiness in her life now her son and daughter were grown, he away with the army like her husband, and she recently married to a banker in Madrid.

CHAPTER 7

Standing to attention on the dusty parade ground, Izil was no longer the dishevelled shepherd in clothes which were frayed and holed. He looked every bit a soldier in his smart khaki uniform and a red fez with a black tassel. The Moroccan Regulares and the soldiers of Spain's Legion in Morocco constituted the Africanistas, thousands of men who formed the backbone of the Spanish army, and one third of its total strength.

If only his father knew that he was to defend the Faith, thought Izil, he would surely change his mind and give his approval. These infidels were no longer like his father believed them to be. He and his fellow soldiers were allowed to pray several times a day and attend the local mosque.

Their commanding officer told the troops Christians and Muslims worshipped the same God, and their sacred duty was to defend both religions from attack by the atheism growing in Spain like a cancer which would spread to Morocco also. The 'rojos', the reds, were godless communists, who would tear down their mosques and burn the

Koran if they weren't stopped, the man warned them.

And not only did Izil now eat three times a day but he'd already been able to send money to his family, more money than they'd ever possessed. Izil smiled while he imagined the delight there must be on their faces, able at last to sit down to meals the likes of which they hadn't enjoyed in years.

That evening, the teenage boy he'd entrusted to take the money into the mountains for a small fee entered Izil's dormitory. In the palm of the boy's hand was the small goatskin purse Izil had given him the day before.

"Your father told me to go away, he didn't want your money."

Izil sighed, he would just have to take it in person when he got some leave in August.

Ramon met Mariela outside the apartment.

"Come, let me show you your home."

Ramon followed her up the two flights of stairs still taking in those words. A place of his own was something he'd never thought about, it was something that had seemed unattainable.

Mariela flung open the shutters, replacing sombre shadow with light. "Take a look, I think you'll like the view."

Below, the River Guadalquivir, named from the Arabic 'al-wadi l-kabir', meaning 'the big river', drifted languidly on its journey to the Gulf of

Cadiz. Prominent on the other bank was the twelve-sided watchtower, El Torre del Oro, which, reflecting its name, shone in the golden glow of the evening sun. 'Tower of gold' was said to be a reference to the city's golden age when ships from Spain's Latin American colonies arrived there to unload their cargoes of gold and silver. Like much of the city, the tower originated from when the Moors had ruled and it looked as fanciful as Arabia.

"What do you think?"

"It's wonderful."

"It can be our love nest. My husband will be home on leave soon so I'll visit you here instead."

Ramon's joy flew out of the open window. Briefly, he'd forgotten the unspoken bargain between them. This apartment wasn't really his home and it never would be. He was merely a guest. When she tired of him or if he wanted to finish the affair, he would need to go.

Their relationship was already beginning to feel wrong to him but Ramon persuaded himself that he mustn't end it. For so long as he didn't need to pay rent, he could send more money home and start putting some aside for Carmelita's operation. And he couldn't deny that satisfying Mariela was pleasurable, even if he felt detached from her in those intimate moments.

Located on a peninsula between the two branches of the Guadalquivir, Triana was grittier than her sophisticated sister on the eastern bank. Here

Ramon discovered the city's underbelly, a district where the less privileged lived, a place for sailors, vagabonds, immigrants, and gitanos. People not wanted and looked down upon, but generally left alone if they remained in Triana.

Mariela visited without notice, usually during siesta, and more often than Ramon hoped she would. He would have pretended to be out but he couldn't. She retained a key and came in to check when he didn't answer, most probably doubting his claims he'd been asleep and hadn't heard her knock.

She was endlessly generous, bringing him numerous gifts. On one occasion, she brought a large package.

"You need to stop, Mariela. You make me feel inadequate."

"It's not for you, it's a dress for your sister."

Ramon blushed. "I'm sorry, I shouldn't be so ungrateful. She'll love it."

Later, they lay in bed, shutters and windows closed as a barrier against the afternoon heat and to preserve the cooler conditions created by the tiled floor and thick walls. A solitary fly buzzed around them, loud and irritating.

Mariela raised her head, supporting it with her right hand, her stare interrogating Ramon's eyes. "You'll want to be rid of me one day, I know you will."

"Maybe you'll want to be rid of me," countered Ramon.

"No, never."

Mariela burst into tears, putting her head in her hands and turning her back on him.

Ramon hugged her. "Don't cry. I'm here, aren't I?" But her crying had failed to move him.

Ramon might not love Mariela but he'd fallen in love. She possessed charms he never tired of. She fizzed with life and satisfied his senses. Her architecture and her señoritas were a feast for the eyes, her guitar players on street corners were melodic to the ear, and her bars and cafes delighted the tongue.

Yet this city of beguiling charm harboured ugly truths. Truths Ramon witnessed in the street fights between strikers and the fascist 'blue shirts', the Falangists.

Walking in Macarena one day, north of the centre, Ramon turned a corner to find a wall of men in uniform blocking the street, their backs to him. On their heads, black hats. Box-like at the front and wider at the rear, they had the appearance of small wings as if the devil's answer to guardian angels. La Guardia Civil, the Civil Guard, were the enforcers of the status quo, protectors of those accustomed to power and unwilling to relinquish any: the Church, the landowners, and the industrialists.

Ramon heard them but couldn't see them. Only banners were visible above the Civil Guards. Chanting voices demanded justice and liberty and sang the 'Internationale', the socialist anthem.

The guards removed the rifles slung over their shoulders. Orders to disperse were shouted, rifles positioned. Footsteps of retreat reverberated off nearby buildings and banners fell from view. Gunshots and screams took the place of singing.

Ramon diverted down a side street and hid in an alley to avoid accusation of involvement. When he emerged later, patches of crimson drying in the sun were the only signs of what had occurred.

Not for the first time, Ramon experienced guilt that he failed to join protests or attend political meetings, a coward who didn't stand up for his beliefs. That road, he told himself, would lose him his job and result in his family going hungry. Yet, his mind answered back, the ogres of unemployment and hunger would always be stalking him so long as he lived unless he was willing to join the struggle and end a system that benefitted only a rich minority.

CHAPTER 8

Mariela's mood swings became frequent and abrupt. Sweetness could change to anger or despair in the blink of an eye.

"Soon no one will want me save for smelly old men." Mariela was seated by the window while she twirled her dyed auburn hair with her fingers, the silk dressing gown which she kept at the apartment loosely draped around her. "I don't want that. I'll kill myself if you leave me.".

Ramon sat up in bed. There was a worrying seriousness of intent in her expression "Don't say that. You have a family."

"Huh, they don't need me anymore. You're all I have." Ramon broke into a sweat. He didn't know how to respond. He couldn't take responsibility for her happiness, obliged to remain her lover to prevent her from taking her own life. His failure to say anything provoked her. "I don't even have you now do I?" Her face crumpled. "I should have kept my big mouth shut, I always spoil things."

Their conversation ended and the lack of it wasn't filled by a kiss or caress. Mariela dressed hurriedly.

"I can't come tomorrow but I'll be here the day after." The matter of fact tone in which she imparted the information ignored what had just happened, as if everything was as it was before.

"I'm going home for a few days," blurted out Ramon. He'd made no plans to do so but he needed to get away from her. "I want to give Carmelita that beautiful dress you gave me."

"When will you be back?"

"Sunday."

"Sunday? That's four days away. Why so long? Are you running away from me?" There was anger in her voice, an unspoken but definite threat of consequences if he didn't return.

Ramon wanted to tell her what he did was none of her business but that wasn't what he said. "I haven't seen my family in over three months. The time will soon pass."

"I'll see you Sunday then."

"But I'll be back late."

"It doesn't matter. I'll be here, waiting."

Ramon smiled, a false smile.

Ramon was seated tall and proud while the bus ascended the twisting road to his village. He had left on foot and in a farmhand's clothes. He was returning by bus, well dressed and well heeled. He'd thrown off worries about returning. There'd be no problems, Ramon assured himself. Villagers he'd known all his life greeted him while he walked along the street.

"My, you look like a duke, Ramon," cried one.

Some merely watched him pass, their vacant expressions witness to the impoverished life people led here.

His mother let out a shriek of surprise when he entered. "My son."

Carmelita looked up and gave him her unique and unusual smile.

"Here, Carmelita, take this."

Reaching inside the paper bag, Carmelita pulled out the dress and held it up in wonder. It was a bright green, the colour of spring grass before it withered in the heat. "It's so beautiful."

"Not as beautiful as my sister," said Ramon embracing her. "And for you, mother."

The box he presented her with was small.

"What is it?"

"Open it."

"Oh, Ramon! My mother's ring. God bless you. How did you survive without selling it?"

Ramon told his family of his time in Seville, omitting that he'd had to pawn the ring and mention of Mariela.

"I always said you'd make us proud. But you can't stay. Didn't you get my letter?" The delight in his mother's face at seeing her only son had surrendered to a frown. "You'll have been noticed, and maybe by one of his paid informers. Francisco Castillo Morales and his men could come for you at any time

"Francisco? What about Don Pedro?" asked

Ramon.

"He was killed, his body found lying in a ditch. No one knows who did it. His henchmen have been terrorising the men in the village to find the culprit. You'd be an easy target for blame or revenge."

Ramon experienced a surge of pleasure to think the tyrant Don Pedro was dead but it was brief. Francisco would be equally as bad, if not worse. A young man eager to show he could fill his father's shoes. "I'll take the bus in the morning."

"No, leave now. You must get away from this village."

"But-"

"Go. There's no need to worry about us. Maybe in time you can send for us and we'll come and live with you in Seville."

Darkness had fallen when Ramon walked out into the night and down the hill. There was only a sliver of a moon but noise carried far. Above the familiar buzzing of the cicadas was a deeper sound, an unwelcome one, the sound of horses' hooves. Ramon left the road and stood behind an olive tree.

"They said he came this way. He can't have got far." Ramon recognised the gruff voice of the Castillo's foreman.

The blackness was illuminated by a powerful light, sweeping in an arc. Ramon held his breath, his body rigid with anxiety. If they saw him, he couldn't outrun them. They were advancing towards him, and any moment now the beam of light would be pointed in his direction. If they came any closer they must surely find him.

Ramon crouched down and ran his hand over the dirt. Locating a fallen branch, he threw it as far as he could. The thump when it landed attracted his pursuers.

"Over there!"

They moved off and he went the other way, deeper into the night. He slept little, alert to every sound and not even dozing until shortly before dawn when he finally lost the battle to keep his eyes open. Once the sun rose, he made his way back to the side of the road and waited for the bus to appear.

CHAPTER 9

Back in Seville by noon, Ramon consoled himself that, despite his trip being curtailed, he would have a few days without Mariela. He was free to do exactly as he wished, a luxury he hadn't experienced since he was a boy.

He made his way across the iron bridge, Puente de Isabel II, and past the striking blue and yellow ceramic dome of Capilla Carmen at the Triana end. A cacophony of market stall holders touting their wares and haggling housewives filled a pungent air smelling of fish while he passed by the lively market where pigs hung on hooks, heads down as if victims of torture.

The market by the river bank stood on the site of what once was the Castle of Gabir, before becoming Castillo de San Jorge when the Muslims surrendered the city. Used as the headquarters of the Spanish Inquisition, its dank dungeons were a place of torture and imprisonment for those accused of being heretics. In particular, Muslims and Jews who had converted to Catholicism to avoid being expelled from Spain.

Sleeping until late afternoon, Ramon then went for a walk through Triana's narrow streets and lost himself in the atmospheric staccato stamping of feet coming from inside several of the buildings. Triana was a spiritual homeland of flamenco.

Under balconies, the attractive tiles, which Triana was famous for producing, caught Ramon's eye. Tiles made here decorated Seville and other Spanish cities in a timeless beauty. So much that was appealing and dramatic about this city originated from this down at heel part of town.

Dusk was approaching, wrapping Seville in a warm embrace and whispering to the inhabitants behind their shutters that the scorching heat of afternoon was waning. They would soon emerge to continue with their day, going back to work until eight, and then maybe meeting friends for a drink and dining around ten. Sevillanos stayed up until the early hours. Sleep could wait until death. Life was for living, not sleeping.

The two of them almost collided when she came out of a shop, not looking where she was going.

Halting, she stared at him. "It's you. The one who defended me." Ramon, too surprised to say anything, merely nodded. "Thank you, it was brave of you."

She continued on her way. Ramon stood glued to the spot, watching her go. She would soon disappear once more as she had that night in the village.

He broke free from his paralysis and ran after her.

"Stop! Wait. I'm Ramon."

"Beatriz. Encantada." Her wide smile encouraged him.

"Would you care for a drink sometime?"

"My family wouldn't approve. But they don't control me," she added. "Meet me in Plaza Doña Elvira in Santa Cruz tonight at nine. You know where that is, right?"

"Yes." Ramon didn't but he could ask.

Santa Cruz was once the city's Jewish quarter. Under Seville's Muslim rulers the Jews had largely thrived, but when Spain's Christian kings conquered the city in the thirteenth century their fate was sealed. Thousands were massacred in anti-Semitic riots. By the end of the fifteenth century a decree expelling them from Spain left no practising Jews in the country, other than a few who hid their faith and pretended to be Catholics.

Santa Cruz's warren of narrow streets opened onto unexpected squares. With its tiled benches under orange trees, Plaza Doña Elvira offered an ideal rendezvous for those who wanted to be discreet.

Ramon arrived early. Sitting down on a bench, he waited. Late, Beatriz appeared from behind him, a black shawl on her head despite the warm night.

Ramon stood up. "Shall we go to that bar over there?"

"No, here is fine. How come you're here in Seville?" she asked as she sat down.

Ramon told his story. "It makes me feel bad that I

was the cause of you having to leave your village," said Beatriz.

"No, you weren't at fault. It was that evil priest who has lorded it over us for so long who's to blame. Anyway, it all turned out for the best. I have a much better life here and can send money home to my family."

"Well, that's good to know. I can't believe that you ended up living close to me, in Triana of all places."

"Me too. I thought I'd never see you again. It's as if it's…" Ramon hesitated to say the word.

"Fate?"

"Yes, fate."

The ice broken, their conversation flowed effortlessly and Ramon lost track of time, enchanted by her deep midnight eyes.

After what seemed only a moment but had probably been over an hour, Beatriz stood up. "It's late, I must go. I'd like to repay you for your chivalry. How would you like to learn flamenco?"

Ramon wasn't really interested in dancing yet it would be an opportunity to see her again. "Yes I'd like that, but I should warn you that I don't have good co-ordination. You'll probably regret your offer."

She laughed. Her laugh was throaty and endearing. "I like a challenge. I'll come to your apartment to teach you. How about if we start tomorrow, early evening?"

"My apartment?"

"Yes, too many tongues would be wagging if we

met in a place anyone might recognise me."

Butterflies fluttered inside Ramon, and he was embarrassed how clammy his hands had become when she took hold of them to demonstrate where his arms should be. The lesson passed in a haze. When it ended, he fully expected not to see her again yet she returned several times.

While they danced their eyes locked, he moving towards her as she moved backwards, she towards him while he backed away, and then a tense moment when they were only a hair's breadth apart but never touching. Ramon wondered if the intensity he saw in her gaze was an indication of how she felt about him or part of the persona she adopted when she danced.

His answer came one evening when a rare summer storm pounded the city. Beatriz had asked him to open the shutters to let in the cooler air. Darkness fell but they didn't turn on the light. Frequent bursts of lightning momentarily illuminated the room and their faces, Beatriz so close to him, her warm breath caressing his face. She stopped dancing but didn't move away like she always had before. Ramon slowly moved his lips towards hers. She removed the clasp on her head and shook it, letting her hair cascade.

Their passion was electricity and as all consuming as flamenco. Afterwards, they lay listening to the pleasing sound of the heavy rain bouncing off the cobbles. They said little but in that single evening all had changed.

Ramon floated to work on a cloud of happiness thinking of the woman of his dreams, ecstatic she was now a reality. He decided he must move out and rent a room to free himself from Mariela. Fortunately, he would have some time to find another place. Mariela was currently down on the coast in Cadiz with her husband for two months to escape the furnace Europe's hottest city became during July and August.

"What's got into you?" asked Señor Gonzalez while Ramon wiped down the counter in the early hours after the bar closed. "You've been grinning from ear to ear all evening. Don't tell me you're in love." Ramon struggled to suppress a grin. "I'll take that as a yes."

Soon Ramon wanted more than the hour Beatriz stayed for when she visited.

"Can you meet me after midnight when I finish work?" He asked while she put up her hair before rushing home. "We can wander through the city and watch dawn rise by the banks of the Guadalquivir."

"I can't. And this, us," Beatriz flung her arms out in emphasis, "it must end."

"End?" A crushing anxiety had taken hold of him. "We've only just begun and you want to finish it?"

"Yes." Her voice cracked with emotion and her eyes became rheumy. "You don't understand. If my father or brother discover what's going on, they will kill you. They'll consider you have dishonoured me. I can't let that happen."

"We can run away. Go to Madrid and start a new life, together."

"But-"

"But what? I love you, Beatriz. If you love me, what more is there to say?"

"I do love you, Ramon, but it's complicated. I need time to think. My family would disown me, forever. And what if you tire of me?"

"Never," insisted Ramon, pulling her close for a kiss.

Beatriz broke free from his embrace. "Give me a couple of days. You shall have my answer then. I must go."

CHAPTER 10

Izil sat up abruptly, woken by gunfire. Instinctively, he grabbed the rifle by the side of his bed.

An officer burst into the dormitory. "On parade!" he bellowed.

"Are we under attack?" asked someone.

"No, traitors had to be dealt with."

"Traitors?"

"Stop asking questions and obey my order."

Hurriedly the soldiers put on their uniforms and ran out into the breaking dawn. An unremarkable man, short in stature with a moustache addressed them. His voice was surprisingly high pitched.

"I am your leader, General Franco." Looking up at the sky, he lifted his arms as though calling upon the heavens for support. "This is a glorious day. We are rising up against the Jews, the Communists, and the Free Masons, to liberate Spain and Morocco from their evil clutches. We have already executed those in our army here who maintained their allegiance to the Reds in Madrid. Today we shall begin an airlift to Seville. In years to come, you will be able to tell your children and grandchildren with pride how you defended your faith from the godless."

Izil's stomach turned over when he jumped down from a truck and marched across the concrete at Tetouan airfield where several aeroplanes waited, their propellors on the nose and wings already whirring like gigantic wasps.

Parts of the Navy hadn't joined the coup against Spain's democratically elected government, so Franco was unable to get his twenty-five thousand troops across the Straits of Gibraltar by ship. Instead, he used aircraft provided by Hitler. For many days, the planes would fly back and forth to Seville several times each day. Designed to carry only seventeen, the seats had been removed to accommodate forty at a time.

Seated on the floor and squeezed against the metal fuselage, Izil couldn't bring himself to look out of the large window next to him. The engines were deafening, adding to his terror. An unpleasant, bitter taste rose in the back of his throat as he fought back vomit when the plane took to the air, bouncing and shaking alarmingly while it climbed. Izil was convinced it must be about to break into a thousand pieces, and visions of plummeting earthwards bombarded Izil.

By the time they reached the coast of Spain, Izil had relaxed a little and looked down in wonder on Al-Andalus, that fabled land which his ancestors had conquered in the eighth century and ruled for hundreds of years. Far below, lay a patchwork of green, brown, and white; a collage of trees, fields, and small towns. Izil imagined Allah might view his magnificent creation from such a vantage point.

"Ramon!" Mariela called out his name in both command and desire when she entered the apartment. Met with silence, she sat down to await his return, imagining their reunion. Mariela couldn't bear to wait until the end of August to see him again so she'd invented an excuse and taken a train to spend the night in Seville.

Hearing footsteps on the staircase, she hid behind the door. She would surprise him. The excitement on her face when she revealed herself was quickly replaced by a louring scowl. "Who are you?"

"I might ask you the same question," shot back Beatriz.

Mariela looked her rival up and down, someone much younger and more beautiful. Mariela understood only guile would see her prevail. "I see you're carrying a suitcase. Moving in or running away?"

"That's none of your business."

"Did Ramon tell you this was my apartment? I thought so. I can see from your expression that he didn't. You're wasting your time, he's gone and he's not coming back."

"That can't be true." But Mariela could tell from Beatriz's eyes she feared it was.

"I'm afraid it is. He told me he couldn't go through with it." Mariela, also battling to control her emotions, had many more years' experience in doing so. She lit a cigarette and confidently exhaled, failing to turn her head to one side to ensure the smoke collided with her rival's face. "You're not the first woman he's let down. I can see you're upset, can I offer you a coffee?" Mariela knew his new lover was most unlikely to accept.

"No, I must go."

Mariela's feelings escaped once the other woman had gone. She'd always known this moment would come, but the intensity of her pain was profound, as if he'd stabbed her in the heart. While she sobbed, she clawed at her chest trying to remove the dagger of loss. Eventually, crying gave way to a different emotion. The cheat, the snake, he'd betrayed her, and after all she had done for him.

Her face creased with bitterness, she made her way to her home. Troops surrounded the Town Hall. Mariela knew what must be happening, her husband had spoken of the need for it many times.

"Ramon, pour a glass of our finest sherry for every customer," said Señor Gonzalez to a background of cheers. "General Queipo de Llano has taken the city. This time the army will succeed."

Hands shaking, Ramon began pouring. To him, the news was terrible and no cause for celebration. He wanted to leave and get away from this nest of Nationalists. If the army succeeded, Spain would be going backwards, back to oppression and hopelessness.

He thought of his mother and sister and worry seized his mind. And already five days had passed but Beatriz hadn't come. She must have decided to stay with her family or maybe her father had locked her in the house. Ramon cursed he didn't know where in Triana she lived. If he did, he could go and see her father, reassure the man his intentions were honourable, ask his permission to propose.

The customers were crammed in a huddle by the far end of the long marble top counter, listening intently to the radio placed there by Gonzalez.

"The rebels are holding out in Triana and Macarena," one told him.

They aren't rebels, thought Ramon. All of you here, you are the rebels, supporting the overthrow of a government elected in a fair vote by the people. Once he'd served the drinks, he waited until they were absorbed once more in their self congratulation and slipped quietly out.

Taking a circuitous route down back streets to avoid checkpoints, Ramon was soon sweating profusely. Damp with perspiration from the heat and anxiety, his shirt clung to him like a wet cloth. He succeeded in crossing the bridge to Triana before the army got there. On the far end of it, a makeshift barrier of cafe tables and chairs had already been thrown up as if detritus washed down river by a flood. Male residents manned it, a few with rifles but many with nothing to defend their homes it seemed but their bare hands.

Ramon raised his arms as he approached. "Don't shoot, I live here. I'm a Republican."

"I recognise him," said one. "Let him through."

"Do you have a weapon at home?" asked another.

"No, unless you consider a kitchen knife to be one."

"It'll have to do, go get it."

Reaching the apartment, Ramon opened the shutters. Their guns blazing and supported by artillery fire, soldiers were advancing across the bridge. By the time he opened the front door to his building, he could see from his view along the street that the barricade had already been breached. Hands rose in surrender. Then, to Ramon's horror, the defenders began falling like dominoes, shot where they stood.

He went back inside. The brutality of the Nationalists was every bit as bad as he feared it would be. Agitated, Ramon bit a finger nail while he considered what to do. He could try to reach his village but that would be putting his mother and sister in danger if he were to be captured there. It would be better to flee and find the front line where he could join the fight for the Republican cause.

CHAPTER 11

"Look," exclaimed Brahim while he and Izil walked towards the cathedral, "even those we are here to fight for fear us, los Moros." Spaniards, unnerved by their darker skin tone and the red fezzes they wore, moved out of their way when the two men approached. "We're still the stuff of their nightmares, a race they believed they'd driven out forever. Isn't it ironic we're back to fight their so-called crusade for them?"

Izil hadn't yet been involved in the fighting. By the time they arrived in Seville, Triana had been taken. Although resistance in the working class district of Macarena was continuing, there was no need for reinforcements. Bombing by aircraft would soon secure victory.

That evening, the Africanistas were permitted to leave their barracks and roam the city. Izil enjoyed the company of Brahim, a Berber from Tetouan, whose education had evidently been superior to his own.

"La Giralda," pointed out Brahim. "It was a minaret when we ruled, and once the tallest building in the world, crowned with four copper balls of decreasing size and topped with the crescent moon. Inside are ramps instead of stairs so the muezzins were able to ride to the top on a horse and call the faithful to prayer."

"How do you know so much?" asked Izil.

"The Imam who taught me was a great scholar and has studied many works on Islamic Spain, some of which he lent me to read. Look how Islamic the arched balconies are, and also the patterned stonework. The mosque was adjacent and converted by the infidels into their cathedral before they built the present one.

"It's a tragedy we lost Al-Andalus. We civilised this heathen land. Nearby Cordoba, which I hope we'll get the chance to visit, became Europe's greatest centre of learning. While Europeans remained mired in ignorance and filth, we founded universities and built libraries and led the world in the study of medicine and astronomy. In Cordoba alone, there were nine hundred public bathhouses. When the Spanish drove us out, they closed them and banned washing. How disgusting is that? At least now we'll get the chance to take vengeance against some of them for our loss, and for their barbaric occupation of our homeland." There was a distinct relish in Brahim's tone at the prospect.

Come early evening, the sound of shooting in Triana had become sporadic. Ramon decided to venture out once more to see what was happening and in the hope he might find Beatriz. A deep anxiety gnawed at his gut that something bad might have happened to her.

Ramon had barely begun his descent when he heard someone ascending the stairs. He retreated into the apartment, gripping the kitchen knife tightly when the handle turned and the door opened.

"Beatriz." He placed the knife on the table. "What's wrong?" Her lips trembled and she fell into his arms sobbing.

"They shot my father and brother. They dragged them out into the street and slaughtered them like animals. Then they made my mother and I come outside. I thought they'd kill us too. The other women of the neighbourhood were there also, women whose menfolk they had murdered in cold blood. They told us we had ten minutes to wash away the Republican and anti-fascist slogans on the walls or we'd be shot. They shouted at us when we cried, and told us there is to be no mourning and that we're forbidden to dress in black. They said there's nothing to mourn because the dead were the enemies of Spain."

"That's so awful," sighed Ramon.

"I had to come to find out if you were still here in Triana, and, if you were, that you were all right. I was frightened about what would become of you if you hadn't already left like the woman said you had." Traumatised, Beatriz clung to him.

Ramon took her head gently in his hands and

raised it from his chest. "The woman?"

"Yes, she was here when I came round earlier. I was ready to run away with you. She said you had gone, gone for good."

"Mariela." Ramon whispered the word and dropped his hands to his side.

"Who is she?"

"Someone I met when I first arrived. She owns this apartment. I soon found out she isn't normal, disturbed you could say. She lied to you, hoping to break us up. We need to leave and get to Republican territory."

Beatriz drew back. "I can't. I can't abandon my mother, not now. You must go though, they'll surely kill you as well if they find you."

"No, I'm not leaving without you," insisted Ramon. Beatriz's eyes became steely with determination. "If you love me, you'll go. If you die here, I'll have nothing left. You need to get away so I can live in the hope that one day when this madness ends we'll be together. Don't take that from me, I beg you."

Ramon fought to hold back tears. "I'll do as you ask. But can you do something for me?"

"Yes, anything."

"When things calm down, and if you can do so without putting yourself in danger, will you go to my village to see that my mother and sister are all right?"

"Of course. I really must go now and get back to my mother. Carry me in your heart, Ramon, until we meet again." Overcome, Beatriz quickly departed.

Ramon slumped into a dining chair and held his face in his hands, unable to believe the terrible reality of today and how in less than twenty-four hours life had forever altered.

He decided to wait until gone midnight before attempting to get out of the city. Long before then heavy boots resounded on the wooden stairs. Two soldiers burst into the room, and after them came a face which Ramon knew. The man recognised him also.

"Hiding like a coward as always," sneered the son of Don Pedro, Francisco Castillo Morales. "Take him."

With his right arm so far up his back, Ramon thought the bone would surely fracture, he was manhandled down the staircase and out into the street. Pushed into the back of a truck already packed with other prisoners, they were driven away at speed.

Their journey was short. At gun point the men were herded onto a ship, the Cabo Carveiro, moored on the Guadalquivir. But cargo ship it was no longer, instead it had become a crowded metal hellhole, an airless oven in Seville's stifling mid-summer temperatures.

Prisoners' details were noted and an 'x2' written on their notes. Each day as new prisoners arrived and the unsanitary conditions became more cramped, others were removed never to return. Instinctively, Ramon and his fellow inmates came to understand what 'x2' meant and what was going to happen, though not where. Those taken were executed by the old city walls.

In the unrelenting heat, which was impossible to escape and sapped the will to live, the days and nights on board passed interminably slowly. There was plenty of time to contemplate how to choose to die and to think of loved ones never to be seen again.

Food was minimal and the drinking water contaminated. The ship was so overcrowded that there wasn't enough room to lie down. Diarrhoea covered the floor on which they were forced to sit when they could endure standing no longer. The all pervasive stench mingled with the hot air and made each breath unwelcome.

The day when a guard called his name, Ramon experienced an unexpected relief that death would soon end this nightmare. He would no longer be condemned to live in this chthonic horror where sleep consisted of only brief dozes of exhaustion and where even night brought no respite from the debilitating heat. Ramon knew he would die like he had lived, a nobody. The only thing he could control was how he died. He'd already decided he would choose to die with defiance and dignity.

CHAPTER 12

In Triana, sapphire skies failed to dispel the fog of fear which stalked the streets. Every evening General Queipo de Llano broadcast on Radio Sevilla, adding to the atmosphere of intimidation. He boasted of capturing Seville with only a handful of men when he had in fact come with a force of thousands. The man swore that for every Franco supporter killed, he would shoot ten Republicans.

As the Nationalist army fanned out across southern Spain to attack areas they didn't yet control, Queipo praised the Regulares, the Moroccan soldiers, "Despite their being foreigners, they have much more love for Spain than all the Marxist scum". And the man struck terror into the female population with his remark, "Many women prisoners have fallen into our hands, the Regulares will be delighted."

Outside on the communal patio, Beatriz and her mother could hear the man ranting on a neighbour's radio.

"Let's go in," said her mother. "I can't bear to listen

to that sadist any longer. I can only pray that on the day of judgment our Lord will decree the punishment he deserves." Beatriz shut the door behind them. "And you, Beatriz, I wonder what the Lord will say to you?" Her mother raised her eyebrows in interrogation.

Beatriz's cheeks turned crimson. "I - I don't know what you mean," she stammered.

"I heard you retching both this afternoon and this morning. Did those fascist pigs rape you?" Beatriz didn't answer while she weighed her reply. "Well, did they or didn't they? It's a simple enough question."

Beatriz lowered her head to avoid her mother's gaze. "I didn't know how to tell you."

"My poor girl." Her mother reached out and placed her hand on her daughter's. Beatriz was surprised by this unexpected show of empathy. Her relationship with her mother had been difficult ever since she'd ceased to be an obedient little girl and pushed for independence from her mother's stifling domination. "No one will want to marry you if you give birth to the bastard growing inside you. But don't worry, I know someone who can take care of the situation. Nobody need ever know."

The thought of terminating her pregnancy horrified Beatriz. Discovering she was carrying Ramon's child had brought joy and melted her heart so frozen with grief. It was something wonderful in a time of such sadness.

"I'll go and talk to the woman tonight, we mustn't delay. I think God will forgive you. You're no longer a virgin, but it wasn't your fault."

Ramon was blindfolded and escorted off the ship and into the back of a truck. In his sightless world, he could see the faces of those he loved: his mother, Carmelita, and Beatriz. While he steeled himself for the inevitable, he fought to keep their images fixed in his mind. He wanted to die remembering them.

When the vehicle came to a halt, Ramon was hauled out. Held under each arm, he was dragged quickly into somewhere. He wondered if they would remove his blindfold before shooting him. He hoped not, it seemed easier not to know when the executioners were about to fire. But they ripped it off.

Ramon squinted and looked around for other victims and the firing squad. There were none. Ramon was in an office. In the shuttered shadows, he could see someone seated at a desk opposite him. It was a face he'd seen only weeks ago, that of Francisco Castillo Morales. The man's feet were casually placed on the desk. With the fingers of one hand he was casually spinning a revolver.

"You are fortunate, you have a friend in high places, the wife of a senior officer who has the ear of the General. Though what she ever saw in you escapes me. The woman is an enigma, first she reports you and now she tries to save you. I'll offer you a choice, Russia or the Legion."

"Russia?" asked Ramon, confused.

Castillo gave a short laugh of contempt. "You really are an ignorant peasant. Russia means death. Death or you fight for the Legion."

Ramon was torn. If he chose to live, he'd be expected to kill his own kind and become a traitor. Castillo removed his feet from the desk and slammed his fist upon it. "Make a choice! I don't have any more time to waste on you. I want you out of here, you smell of shit." He stood up, pointing his gun at Ramon. "Death it is then."

"The Legion," blurted out Ramon.

"That's a pity, I was looking forward to killing you myself. Still, you won't last long in battle, that's for sure. Get him out of here."

Ramon pushed the arms away that came for him. "I have only one request. Please don't harm my mother and sister, they are innocent."

"What happens to them is of no interest to me, but they're both such ugly bitches I doubt the Africanistas will want to rape them when they take the village."

Ramon wanted to leap across that desk and pummel Castillo to a pulp, yet once again he was powerless. To attempt such a thing would surely enrage the man so much that he would make a point of seeing that his mother and sister were killed and in a most horrible fashion. The soldiers yanked him by the arms and steered him out.

Later that day, Ramon stood with several other

men in their soiled civilian clothes in the square of the high-walled barracks while an officer from the Legion shouted at them.

"Right, you miserable excuses for Spaniards, it's my misfortune to have to train you. And don't think you can get away with not fighting. Any of you who I deem to be failures will meet your original fate. And once out there, you won't be able to shirk your duty. You'll be out front, our cannon fodder. Try and escape and we'll shoot you down like the vermin you are."

Ramon thought choosing death by firing squad would, in hindsight, have been the better option but reminded himself that so long as he could stay alive there was hope. Hope that one day he would see Beatriz and his family again.

They were given uniforms and photographed, a permanent record of their betrayal of the Republican cause. The training was basic, it seemed clear they weren't intended to survive for any length of time.

Beatriz's mother was dismissive of her daughter's arguments.

"What others who've been raped might do is irrelevant, that is up to them and their families. I know what your father would have wanted, and it's what I want too."

"I can't murder my own baby," protested Beatriz, standing before her mother seated on a dining chair.

The woman leaned forwards, her hands on her knees, her look stern. "That baby would be a daily reminder of what happened. His father murdered our own kind, maybe even your own dear father and brother. How can you even contemplate dishonouring their memory like that."

Beatriz wanted to tell her mother the truth but she couldn't. Her mother would be outraged to know she'd had sex outside of marriage and, even worse, with someone who wasn't a gitano.

Her mother raised her right hand and wagged her index finger at her daughter. "We've been discussing this for days. I won't hear another word. My contact will be here in the morning. Once it is done, I never want to talk of it again. You wear me out, I'm going to bed."

Waking before dawn, Beatriz listened to her mother snoring while she dressed. She took a ring from a drawer and slipped it on her finger. Quietly as a cat, she slipped out into a moonless night. Beatriz thought of Ramon while she navigated the soundless streets of Seville, interrupted only by the occasional bark of a dog. Reaching the bus station, she sat down on a bench waiting for the sun to rise and the world to wake.

CHAPTER 13

Izil soon became battle hardened, impervious to pleas for mercy. He was accustomed to killing goats. Once you'd killed your first it was easy, and so it was with humans.

His regiment pushed westwards, chanting Islamic prayers to praise the Prophet Mohammed while they advanced. On seeing them approach, those who'd been taught since childhood to consider Moors cruel and barbaric demons often fled without fighting. The Regulares lived up to their reputation, killing all that resisted. Their Spanish overlords had ordered them to do so. The Moroccans fought like lions, unafraid of death because they were confident that should they die they would be going to paradise. This was a Jihad, a war against unbelievers.

After taking a town, their commanders gave them free rein for a couple of hours to do as they wished. Some used the time to rape, others looted property, and some found time for both. Izil and Brahim focussed on collecting artefacts which they could sell, breaking down doors and removing all the valuables they could carry, such as clocks and jewellery. Enterprising merchants at the rear would offer to take the loot off their hands, and after much haggling a deal would be done.

"Doesn't it feel good to finally get our own back after centuries of being looked down upon as no better than animals?" said Brahim while they sat one evening counting their money in the square of a town. Bodies still lay where they had fallen but they ignored them and the swarms of flies. "With luck, the Spaniards will so exhaust themselves fighting each other that after it's all over they won't have the strength to fight us. Then, when we get back to Morocco, we can drive them out and claim our independence, in the North at least."

"Won't the French then move up from the South and take control of all of Morocco if that happens?" asked Izil.

"Maybe, but I've heard talk of war coming to Europe, of a man called Hitler in Germany. He's helping Franco, using him as a trial run to practice his tactics. They say he'll probably start a European-wide war like the first one. If he attacks France, the French may well have to pull out of Morocco to defend their own country. We are living in exciting times, Izil. This is our time, our time to reclaim what is rightfully ours."

Beatriz twisted the ring on her finger while the bus left Seville. Looking at her reflection in the window, she saw herself as others didn't. Her veneer of confidence was like walking on stage to perform, an act.

Beatriz remembered how as a little girl she'd idolised her father. He was her defender and protector. How shattering it had been to discover the real man when she grew to be a teenager. That awful night in their wagon when he sent her brother on an errand. Her father's touch hadn't been gentle and paternal but intrusive and feral. Beatriz defended herself in the only way she was able to.

"We were attacked," her father told her brother on his return, blood dripping from the knife wound across his face. Beatriz too carried a scar from that night, though it was one which nobody else could see.

She mourned her brother, but not her father. Since that day, the man had ceased to be deserving of her love and respect. Keeping her terrible secret and never telling her mother was suffocating, and now Beatriz carried another secret which she had to hide from her. Running seemed the only option. When the bus dropped her and pulled away, Beatriz inhaled deeply. She was about to find out if they were still here, and how they would react to her asking to stay if they were.

There was a solemnity in the village similar to that in Triana, of dreams dashed and hopes crushed, and a sense of unbearable heartache. Malevolence had won, hanging oppressively in the heat of the day. Villagers didn't greet her. Their stares were hollow, those of the haunted and downtrodden.

His home wasn't hard to find. Moaning in the hot wind, the door swung on its hinges. Beatriz knocked and waited and then knocked again. She pushed, opening the door fully. Rays of sunlight fell upon a young woman crouched on her haunches in the far corner. She looked up and Beatriz moved back in surprise. Ramon hadn't told her about his sister's disfigurement.

"Are you Carmelita?" The woman nodded. "I'm Beatriz, Ramon's wife."

"Wife?" Carmelita repeated the word with incredulity.

"Yes, I realise it must be a surprise. We were going to come together to tell you and your mother, but he was in danger and he had to leave and go north. Is your mother out?"

"They took her, they took many. They never came back."

Beatriz tried to ignore Carmelita's strange voice and concentrate on what she was saying. Her words were spoken without emotion. Beatriz wasn't sure if that was because her affliction robbed her of intonation or whether she was still in shock. Perhaps it was a combination of both.

"I'm so sorry."

"We hoped Ramon would send for us but he never did."

Beatriz looked around the room. Carmelita had nothing, no food and no possessions. Beatriz quickly concluded a life here would be impossible and changed her plan.

"He sent me instead. I'd like you to come back to Seville with me."

A solitary tear escaped from the corners of Carmelita's eyes.

In the back of an army truck heading northwest, Ramon was squashed together with others who were also seeking to prolong their lives, even if only for a few days. Conversation was infrequent, they were concentrating on trying to avoid being thrown about while they bounced along a rutted dirt road. Ramon had already twice slammed his head against the metal bars which held the canvass roof in place.

That night they were to sleep in the open on the rock-hard ground guarded by changing shifts of Regulares.

"They have orders to shoot you dead if you try and get away," gloated an officer on their arrival. "If you need to relieve yourselves, you go where you are."

Ramon observed their two guards. Izil and Brahim stared back, forcing Ramon to look away. Their hostile glare indicated they would have no hesitation in following their orders.

Ramon became distracted by the smell of cooking. The delicious aroma of goat meat floated through the evening air. He hadn't eaten since yesterday and his nostrils twitched in anticipation. Yet, as he was soon to discover, such food wasn't for the likes of him. Stale bread was all that was chucked at the men, made worse when Ramon watched the two guards bite into their hunks of meat. When they'd finished, one of them threw Ramon the bone that remained as if he were a dog, and in their eyes he was no better than one, a godless infidel. Ramon ignored the bone and curled up on the ground willing sleep to come and grant him a few hours release from this purgatory.

A deep throbbing from above woke him the next morning. Overhead, German bombers passed on route to their target.

The men were ordered to advance to Badajoz, a town close to the Portuguese border. Miraculously, despite being in the vanguard of the attack, Ramon survived unscathed. He remembered little of the battle. It was a blur. Shouting, smoke, explosions. But one thing stuck vividly in Ramon's mind. It wouldn't allow him to sleep that night. The face of a young Republican soldier.

Clambering over the rubble which had previously formed part of the old city walls, Ramon found himself only metres from the man raising his rifle to fire. Ramon charged and shot first. His speed saved him, but now guilt overwhelmed Ramon. He'd killed someone who believed in what Ramon did, someone who should have been his comrade. Someone who, unlike Ramon, had the courage to die for what he believed in. Ramon was no longer only a coward, he was a murderer too.

CHAPTER 14

Beatriz asked Carmelita to wait outside for a moment, but she could hear the raised voices from within.

"Where on earth have you been?" demanded Beatriz's mother. "I've been worried sick."

"I had to go and fetch someone. My husband's sister."

"Your what!" The exclamation was one of fury.

"I was frightened to tell you because of how you'd react."

"How did you expect me to react? You got married without telling me. To who?"

"His name is Ramon. I kept it a secret because he's not a gitano, and I feared what Papa would do when he found out. Ramon had to flee, the Nationalists would have killed him if he stayed in Seville."

"So you let me believe you'd been raped? How could you."

"Because I knew you'd be like this. My baby came from love, and I'm keeping it."

Carmelita raised her head in surprise, quickly

lowering it again when she noticed passers-by giving her that look strangers always gave her when they noticed her mouth. She smiled for the first time in a long while. She was going to be an aunt. She would have a part of her brother to love and cherish.

From inside, the arguing continued. "How do I know you even married the man, and you're not just a whore? If you can lie to me about being raped, you can lie to me about anything."

Beatriz deflected her mother's question. "There's something else I've never told you. It's something Papa told you I didn't dare contradict, about how he acquired the scar on his face."

Beatriz must have lowered her voice because Carmelita couldn't hear the rest of the conversation. Shortly afterwards, Beatriz opened the door and invited her in. Beatriz's mother was seated on a dining chair. They had no other chairs, but even dining chairs were a luxury to Carmelita who came from a home where you sat on the floor. The wan colours of emotional trauma were etched on the woman's face. Still reeling from her daughter's revelations, she barely reacted to Carmelita's entrance, not even her appearance. Instead, she ignored Carmelita's 'Buenas tardes, Señora' and stared straight through her as if she wasn't there. Carmelita could see the woman bore strong similarities to Beatriz, though her mother's features were less fine. Her nose was wider and her fingers stubby, yet she too must have turned heads when younger.

"Let's go and sit in the courtyard," said Beatriz. She opened the door at the back of the room which led to an enclosed tiled patio shared with surrounding houses. In the centre stood a mature orange tree. They sat down on the tiled floor in the shadow which the tree cast. Carmelita was awed by the beauty of the spot and the beauty of her brother's wife.

"I have something to tell you," began Beatriz.

"I already know, you were both talking rather loudly. It's wonderful news. Does Ramon know?"

"No. When he left, I hadn't found out I was pregnant."

"What will you call the baby?"

"Ramon if it's a boy and Ramona for a girl."

"Oh, that's lovely. I'm so happy Ramon met you and found love."

"Thank you. I hope you will too."

"How could anyone ever love this face?"

Beatriz took Carmelita's hands in hers. "One day I'm going to get the money to pay for the operation you need."

"That's kind of you but you must keep your money for the baby."

"I'll find enough for us all, don't you worry."

Carmelita didn't see how Beatriz possibly could but she was grateful someone cared.

In the central square of Badajoz, Ramon lay on his back amongst those who had escaped to the world of dreams, dreams which surely must be better than their reality.

Ramon knew what he must do. A red dawn breaking above reminded him that the cost of the bargain he'd made to extend his life would be measured in the blood of his own kind. If they shot him in the back while he ran so be it. It was better to die than continue to lead a traitor's life to save only himself.

Soon the sun would reach down into every alleyway and give his hunters unbeatable odds. Ramon was unarmed. At night, the Moors confiscated their weapons in case they should rebel.

Forced to fight to avoid execution, the conscripted men had certainly seen enough to make them want to rebel. The battle's aftermath was even more horrific than the battle itself. Franco's soldiers indulged in an orgy of killing. Rumours spread that hundreds of inhabitants were being rounded up and taken to the city's bull ring to be machine gunned. A rumour that seemed to be confirmed by intermittent bursts of heavy gunfire. At dusk the previous evening, cartloads of corpses heaped on one another coming from that direction to be taken out of the city for burning provided proof of the start of a massacre. Four thousand, one tenth of the city's population, were slaughtered by troops led by the ruthless General Yagüe, who would come to be known as the butcher of Badajoz.

Ramon rolled over onto his stomach. Slithering along the ground, he slowly made his way past sleeping comrades to the point nearest an alleyway. He lay still, his heart thumping but not through exertion.

Like a spring released, Ramon leapt to his feet and sprinted. He ignored the eruption of shouting behind, to turn would waste precious time. A bullet bounced off a wall next to him. The next also failed to hit him and he turned a corner.

Ramon had no idea where he was going. He could be running straight into the arms of his captors. His footsteps resounded in the narrow street, calling out his location. He took refuge behind the pillar of an archway. Ramon's pursuers came thundering down the street and he held his breath. If they stopped and conducted a search there was no way they would miss him. Luckily for him, Izil and Brahim raced on.

Ramon emerged and went down another street. Seeing a river at the far end, he made for it. Ramon was within touching distance of the water when a searing pain in his left calf caused him to fall face first into the river.

CHAPTER 15

Clutching at rocks on the bottom, Ramon pulled himself along the riverbed. He forced himself on until he could no longer ignore his lungs' demand for air. Breaking the surface, he fully expected to be shot at. Ramon snatched a breath and went under once more.

The next time he rose up, he listened. All was quiet. A sudden and unexpected commotion startled him. In a flurry of flapping wings, several ducks took to the air. Peace returned and, seeing no sign of pursuers, Ramon crawled along the river bank until he had left Badajoz behind.

The first time he stood, his left leg buckled. Blood continued to flow and his world became blindingly bright and out of focus. Removing his shirt, Ramon tore off a sleeve and tightly tied it above his wound. He sat on the ground and rested until he no longer felt faint and his vision returned to normal.

Limping, he began to cross the scorched, unforgiving land of Extremadura. A place of such harsh aridity it had driven away those of its native sons born with ambition. Cortes, the conqueror of the Aztecs and Mexico, and Pizarro, the conqueror of the Incas and Peru, had both come from here, Spain's remotest and poorest region.

In a sky lacking a single wisp of cloud to bring relief from the scorching heat, the sun burned with a white hot intensity. Ramon scanned his surroundings constantly. Unable to run, he needed to ensure he wasn't noticed.

Halting for a rest, he observed a lizard only a couple of metres away dart across the surface of a rock and then lie perfectly still upon it. Its thin black tongue, which it pushed out every few moments, gave it away. Spellbound, Ramon watched an eagle dive from above, talons outstretched. The bird grabbed the reptile and soared skywards. Out here Ramon knew he was that lizard, liable to be seized at any moment.

He stumbled on, perspiration dripping from his forehead ran in rivulets down his face, and his tongue became straw in his parched mouth.

Ahead, two flags fluttered in the oven-like breeze. The nearest one bore the three horizontal stripes of Spain, red and yellow but not the purple of the Second Republic. The bottom stripe was red, the flag of the Nationalists. Ramon assumed the other flag, red and green, must be that of Portugal. Luck had brought him tantalisingly close to the border.

He sank into bone dry grass which pricked his bare arm and surveyed the scene. Two soldiers guarded the Spanish side. The stillness was broken by the rumble of a vehicle from the direction of Badajoz. Three soldiers jumped out. Not long afterwards, the border post rose and people appeared and crossed into Spain, their hands on their heads to be herded at rifle point into the truck.

Ramon swallowed, his throat dry not only from lack of water but the knowledge he had gained. Portugal was clearly no sanctuary for those fleeing Franco's brutality. Yet he didn't know where else to go. From what he'd heard, all of western Spain was already under Nationalist control.

Come nightfall, Ramon broke cover. He went north, going beyond the border post and eventually turned west and crossed into Portugal.

Daybreak revealed a landscape every bit as barren as Extremadura. Exhausted and in pain, Ramon sought refuge amongst a grove of cork trees. Their trunks were an unexpected hallucinatory orange after a recent harvesting of their bark. He promptly fell into a deep sleep

"Espanhol?" A wizened face of baked leather and grey stubble was looking down on him, a man who looked every bit as poor as the farm workers of Spain.

Back at his one room dwelling, lacking in any comfort or possessions and reminding Ramon of home, the man, a knife in hand, pointed at Ramon's wound. Ramon fought not to flinch and cry out in agony when the man got to work to remove the bullet.

Afterwards the man began talking. Although his

pronunciation was so different, the words he spoke proved to be similar to Spanish. He mouthed them slowly and repetitively, enabling Ramon to understand. Others who'd escaped from Badajoz were nearby.

At dusk, the man led him to a stone wall behind which five men were gathered. Dishevelled like Ramon, dirt engrained in their skin, dust in their hair, beaten but not defeated.

"Did you come from Badajoz too?" asked one. Ramon nodded. "Are you from there?"

"No, Seville. I was given the choice of death or joining the Legion. I escaped."

"For now. Salazar, Portugal's dictator, is a supporter of the Nationalists. He fears his own regime is at risk if Spain's elected government wins, and that he'll face an uprising should democracy in Spain survive. He's anti-socialist and pro-Catholic like Franco's lot. They say he's allowing the Germans to send arms and men through Portugal. Fortunately, the locals around here are friendly. They suffer under the same system as we do, a few wealthy landowners and crushing poverty for the rest. But we still need to be careful, one of them might be tempted to give us away for a bribe. My name's Miguel."

"Ramon. Do you have a plan?"

"To reach Lisbon and get out on a ship, and then find a way to get to the Republican zone in Spain so we can rejoin the fight."

"Is Lisbon far?"

"It's a long walk but better than the short one back to Badajoz and a firing squad."

The other men with Miguel chuckled at his gallows humour. Ramon laughed too, he was no longer alone.

They made their way west, resting in the shade of olive groves during the day. When not asleep, Ramon thought of Beatriz and his family. Not knowing what had happened to them burrowed into his soul like a parasite. He might be safe but were they?

Peasants who found them were generous, returning with bread they couldn't really afford to share. Whenever they mentioned Salazar and Franco, they spat on the ground.

At night the men walked west, avoiding villages and towns.

Ramon was still limping. He worried if he was destined to always be this way. If he didn't recover he would be of little use for fighting, and when the war ended of incapable of physical labour, unable to make a living and provide for those he loved.

CHAPTER 16

Izil's circumstances had changed in a way he never could have envisaged. A month after Badajoz, they'd conquered Toledo. Franco had been named Generalissimo, recognised above all the other generals. Soon afterwards he was bestowed with the title El Caudillo, or leader.

Izil was no longer fighting. In a white turban and a billowing white cloak, beneath which he wore his uniform, he was seated astride a handsome brown stallion accompanying Franco's official car as they entered a Nationalist controlled town to rapturous adulation. The flag of the Nationalists festooned every building, and admirers watching the procession thrust out their arms in the fascist salute.

Izil was now a member of La Guardia Mora, the Moorish Guard. The guards on their horses flanked each side of Franco's open top car with more in front and at the rear.

It was a contradictory sight. Franco was the self-proclaimed saviour of the Catholic Church in Spain. The man claimed the civil war was a holy crusade like that conducted by Ferdinand and Isabella, who in the late fifteenth century ended the last vestige of Islamic rule in Spain. Yet Franco had chosen Muslims to protect him.

Izil didn't concern himself with such thoughts. He was enjoying his new life of pageantry a great deal more than being a frontline soldier. He pushed his shoulders back with pride, proud of his personal achievement and proud of his heritage.

Izil owed his promotion to an incident in Toledo. Franco came to bask in the glow of victory, photographers in attendance, capturing the moment for posterity. None of them noticed a shadow travelling across rubble, a portent of danger. A sniper in position, taking aim, ready to assassinate, take down El Caudillo right in front of those fawning upon him. Reacting quickly, Izil shot the sniper before he could fire. Izil's reward was an invitation to join Franco's elite guard.

In Seville, Beatriz's tummy grew and so did the gap between mother and daughter. Her mother hadn't taken to Carmelita.

"That girl's nothing but a burden," she complained while she vigorously chopped up an onion that with a couple of eggs would be their meal for the day. "It's enough of a struggle to feed the two of us. She brings nothing, only takes. You should have left her where you found her. She'll bring us bad luck with that face of hers."

"Shush! She might hear you."

"I don't care. Maybe if she does, she'll do the decent thing and leave."

Outside on the patio, Carmelita hung her head. During siesta, while mother and daughter slept, she went out, crossing Puente de Isabel into Seville. She chose la Iglesia Colegial del Divino Salvador, the Church of the Divine Saviour. Built upon the remains of Ibn Adabba, which had been Seville's largest mosque, it looked large enough to offer promise. Inside, the air was refreshingly cool after the punishing walk across the city in the fierce afternoon sun.

She got down on her knees and prayed. Carmelita still venerated the Catholic Church like her mother always had, despite the Church supporting Franco. The sheer magnificence of this house of worship compared to the one in her home village served to awe her more. Supporting columns and vaults of light-coloured stone made it bright and welcoming. The baroque interior and more gold than Carmelita had ever imagined to exist was a thing of sheer wonder, an affirmation for her of God's omnipotence.

After praying, she lit a candle for her mother and then sat down on a pew to wait. On arrival, the priest genuflected before the altar. When he made for a side door, Carmelita hurried over to him, battling her nerves. Confidence and the ability to display it was something she had never possessed.

"Padre."

"Yes, my child."

His lack of reaction to how she looked or sounded reassured her, and her belief that she couldn't do this and should leave immediately, lessened.

"I'm in need of work to help my family. I was wondering if you or someone else you know needs a cleaner. I've cleaned a priest's house before and I'm a hard worker." Carmelita listened to herself speak, that hollow, monotone sound, and lost that brief moment of confidence.

The priest rubbed his chin in contemplation. "I might know someone. Come back tomorrow at the same time."

Carmelita clasped her hands together with gratitude. "Oh thank you, Padre."

Two days later, in Calle de Placentines, a narrow street running north from La Giralda, Carmelita waited outside the imposing double wooden doors which were twice her height. The woman who opened one of the doors was immaculately attired in a dress and short jacket made from silk and as orange as Seville's fruit. Her hair was neatly coiffured and her face reflected a life of privilege, pale and unblemished like an aristocrat from an El Greco painting.

Inside, patterned tiles led to an iron door of intricate filigree through which Carmelita could make out a courtyard of large plants and hear the soft babbling of a fountain, an oasis of quiet and seclusion only metres from the hustle and bustle outside. A method of living the Berbers introduced to Spain when they had conquered it twelve hundred years earlier.

"In here." Carmelita followed the woman into a grand room with a high ceiling and large paintings on the walls and sturdy furniture of dark wood. The lady of the house perched herself on a chaise longue, leaving Carmelita to stand like a child about to be admonished. Carmelita wondered what age the woman must be. Despite her air of self assurance, she looked only to be in her early twenties.

"Tell me of your experience."

"I-"

"Raise your head, I can hardly hear you. In my house, you don't need to be embarrassed about how you look or sound. In my eyes, it gives you an advantage. My husband can be...how shall I put it...easily distracted by beautiful women. I'm looking for someone who will be invisible to him."

Carmelita wanted to cry. She knew to others she was ugly, a freak of nature, but it still hurt when people commented on it. But cry she couldn't, only when she was alone and no one would see. She swallowed hard.

"I cleaned a priest's house for many years, and-"

"Perfect, I'll give you a trial."

Carmelita could hardly believe how brief the interview had been and that she was to be given a chance. "Thank you so much. You won't regret it, I promise."

"Are you in mourning?" The woman didn't give

Carmelita the opportunity to answer. "Wear it for your work. Black is well suited for that also. You may go now. Be here at eight tomorrow and I'll give you the list of your duties which I have prepared." She detected a sudden panic in Carmelita's eyes. "You can't read, can you. No matter, I'll tell you what they are. I prefer it that way. I won't have to worry about you reading things which don't concern you."

"I've found a job so I no longer need be a burden," announced Carmelita when she returned to Triana.

"Congratulations, that's wonderful." Beatriz embraced her. Beatriz's mother offered no words of encouragement and her face remained ice cold. "Let's celebrate," said Beatriz. "I'll teach you flamenco." Her mother tutted with annoyance and left the room.

Carmelita was seized by panic at the thought of being the centre of attention. "But I've never danced in my life."

"So? First, you need to be dressed correctly. We were a similar size you and I, though I can no longer fit into my dancing clothes thanks to this baby."

From the antique cupboard where her costumes were kept, Beatriz produced a teal coloured flamenco dress with the classic tight bodice and ruffles on the lower half. "Come on, it's time you lived a little."

Sheepishly, Carmelita removed her shapeless black dress. She stood as if turned to stone in her shabby underclothes. Once white, they were now a greyish colour with age.

"Step into it." Beatriz helped her pull the dress up and button it. "Now for your hair." Beatriz pulled the ends of Carmelita's short hair which didn't even reach her shoulders and tied it back as best she could. "You look beautiful." That was a word nobody had ever said to Carmelita, other than her brother, and once more she fought to hold back the tears. "Come look in the mirror."

Carmelita shook her head. She had never looked in a mirror after doing so once at the priest's house in the village. Carmelita was so horrified by the face which looked back at her she'd sworn she would never do it again.

Beatriz didn't press her. Instead, she took Carmelita by the hand. "Let's go out onto the patio and get started."

Under the tuition of Beatriz, Carmelita began to discover a joy and a freedom the likes of which she had never experienced. While she danced, she raised her head and welcomed the sun onto her face. Carmelita felt like the seventeen year old she was, glad to be alive and not held prisoner by her appearance. In that moment, for the first time Carmelita could remember, she wasn't ashamed of who she was.

After Beatriz went inside, Carmelita stayed out on the patio looking up at the stars until almost dawn.

She wondered if Ramon was looking at the same infinite sky. She hoped he would be proud of his sister if he could see her now.

CHAPTER 17

Ramon and the other fugitives were within a few kilometres of Lisbon. In between the gaps in its hilly outline of terracotta roof tiles, the crenellated walls of the castle, and church cupolas, they could see their hoped for escape route, the broad River Tagus, its waters mingling with the tides of the Atlantic Ocean.

Evading detection in the hinterland had been relatively easy. The capital city presented a more challenging proposition. Their hosts, a family who lived on the outskirts of Lisbon, informed them that Salazar's secret police were everywhere in the capital. Their webs of detection were numerous, alert to the vibrations outsiders made. If stopped by police, being sent back to Franco's Spain and execution would be inevitable. Santiago, the adult son, volunteered to go down to the port to investigate.

"There's a vessel from Mexico docked," he reported triumphantly on his return.

"Mexico," repeated Miguel, unimpressed.

"Yes, the only Spanish speaking country which has

come out against Franco. If you can get on board, they're unlikely to throw you off."

"But we want to stay in Europe so we can get back to Spain and fight."

"I know, and that's where it gets even better. The ship's sailing for Barcelona which is in the Republican zone."

The faces of the men became animated with excitement, their trek was almost over and a successful outcome within reach.

"When does it leave?"

"Midnight. I'll lead you down there."

They set off once the sun set. The buildings of the city folded around them and Ramon felt as vulnerable as a fly stuck to a spider's web sending out those vibrations. Street lamps diffused light over a wide area. The men walked in twos, apart from Ramon who followed alone at the rear. Sweat dripped from his armpits and trickled down his torso, the tickling sensation causing him to wriggle every few steps. All were conscious their scruffy appearance would mark them out as suspicious.

Above them, lightning broke up the sky and thunder boomed like artillery fire. It began to rain heavily. They made it to the port entrance. Perhaps the secret police didn't like getting wet, thought Ramon.

In the downpour, the lights of the Mexican freighter were a glistening prize. Its engines hummed reassuringly and the metallic smell of fuel drifted towards them. A gangway went up to the deck. Towards the rear of the vessel was a wooden plank leading to an opening in the hold. With a hand signal, Miguel told them to go towards. Still limping, Ramon lagged some way behind.

The sound of splashing and a skid of tyres on puddles caused the men to stop and turn. All save Ramon were illuminated in the headlights of two vehicles. Armed men jumped out, angrily yelling. Ramon dived behind a wooden crate.

He couldn't follow the dialogue, but through gaps in the wood he could see it was going badly. Santiago's attempt to be their spokesperson was failing. The secret police were gesticulating aggressively, demanding responses from Ramon's colleagues to questions delivered in rapid Portuguese which they didn't understand. Moments later they were bundled at gunpoint into the cars and driven off into the night.

Ramon remained where he was, glued by terror. They'd agreed they would all stay together and fight together, and die together if that was to be their fate, brothers in arms. Those men had become Ramon's friends. They'd been in sight of their goal. Yet now, in an instant, they were gone, forever.

It made Ramon think once more of his mother and Carmelita and Beatriz. That voice in his head which he'd always tried not to listen to, a voice which told him he was never going to see them again, was refusing to shut up. Weighed down by the complete unravelling of his life during the last few months, Ramon's legs became lead, not wanting to move another metre. He began snivelling and soon he was wracked by crying that came from deep inside him.

Releasing his pent up emotions improved his mood. He could just give up, Ramon told himself, or stop wallowing in self pity and get on with it. For certain, if he gave in to that negative inner voice, he wasn't ever going to see the faces of those he loved.

Getting to his feet, Ramon limped across to the opening in the hold and entered a world of painted metal and pipes. Finding a hiding place, he stretched out and let sleep temporarily liberate him.

A change in the pitch of the engines and a shuddering woke him. The vessel was pulling away from the dock.

It was the first time Carmelita had been allowed into the room.

"My husband's most particular about his study. Make sure everything goes back in exactly the same place. I'll leave the key in the door. Lock it when you leave and give it back to me."

Carmelita scrupulously adhered to her employer's instructions, taking the utmost care to do exactly as told. When Carmelita picked up a framed wedding photograph of the happy couple to dust she almost dropped it, but it wasn't because she didn't have a good hold of the frame. Her hands trembling, she put it back in its place.

It was him, it had to be. Carmelita had known that face a long time, and after what had happened this summer she could never forget it. The day was seared into her mind as if she'd been branded with a hot iron.

Feeling dizzy, Carmelita sat down on the chair next to his desk. That awful day exploded in her head once more. She pushed her knuckles into her mouth to muffle sobs and stop the Doña coming to investigate.

Carmelita's mind replayed the memory. The unexpected noise of a vehicle on their backstreet, their rickety door kicked open. A man, his face contorted with rage. The man shaking her mother, demanding to know where Ramon was. He refused to believe she didn't know, and slapped her so hard across the face that she fell to the floor.

"Lie to protect your son if you want! We'll take you instead." Nodding at the two men with him, they dragged her mother out by the arms before she was able to stand.

He'd thrown Carmelita a look of contempt. "You're not worth bothering with, you can stay here and starve."

Going outside, Carmelita was already too late. The truck was in motion and accelerating, leaving behind only the acrid smoke of its exhaust.

Carmelita forced herself to continue with her

chores and confine her discovery to the farthest recesses of her mind. Yet while she walked back to Triana that afternoon, she could think of nothing else.

The Doña had never given her name to Carmelita, and the priest had only referred to her as an 'important lady' in need of a cleaner. Now Carmelita knew her name, Doña Castillo Morales, the wife of Francisco. There'd been talk in the village earlier in the year of him getting married but to who, and where they would live, she hadn't known, until now.

Francisco might be at the house one day. He was surely bound to recognise her, yet Carmelita needed to earn money. Beatriz wasn't going to be able to dance, not for months. And when born, Ramon's child would need things which the war had made so expensive. Jobs were hard to find. If Carmelita quit, the chances of finding another were more than slim. She wouldn't be first choice, not with her appearance. By the time Carmelita crossed the bridge into Triana, she had already decided she didn't have a choice.

"Are you all right?" asked Beatriz when Carmelita walked in. "You look pale."

"I'm fine, I just got overly hot walking back."

CHAPTER 18

After several hours at sea, Ramon decided to reveal himself. Reaching the deck, a stiff breeze barrelled into him. He wobbled and grabbed the guardrail. Cresting waves of a dark and impenetrable blue raised the ship and then abruptly dropped it. Ramon had never been out on the ocean before, had never even set eyes upon it until yesterday. Its enormity, stretching uninterrupted to the horizon, was astonishing and made him feel small and alone.

It wasn't long before he was accosted and taken up to the bridge. The captain was unperturbed by the stowaway.

"My government supports your cause, that's why we're taking supplies to Barcelona. You must join me for dinner tonight. A government official who's travelling with us will be most interested to learn of what you have seen. Meanwhile, Fuentes here will show you to a cabin which you may use for the rest of the journey. And I'll ask the medical officer to look at that leg of yours."

Ramon could hardly believe the warmth of his

reception and the luxury he was to enjoy over the next two days. He hadn't slept in a bed or had access to running water for months. They were things whose absence he hadn't often thought about in his village, but after becoming accustomed to them in Seville he missed them. The prospect of a decent meal was yet another unexpected delight.

The government official was an earnest man who refused the offer of wine and seemed uncomfortable in company, a man who preferred his paperwork to conversation.

"The Republicans have few friends, other than us and the Russians," he told Ramon, keeping his head down and avoiding eye contact. "It's most disappointing that Britain and France stick to the non-intervention agreement they promoted when Mussolini and Hitler are ignoring it and giving enormous help to Franco. If Franco is victorious, the cause of democracy in Europe will be further undermined. And the United States doesn't seem prepared to provide assistance. The politicians there are frightened of upsetting Catholic voters."

"Do you think Franco is going to win?" asked Ramon.

"That's something my government has sent me to investigate."

Back in his cabin, Ramon's thoughts returned to his lost colleagues and his family and Beatriz. The sadness of separation was always stronger at night when his mind wandered the avenues of the past, finding only closed doors. Tonight, that feeling was increased by the movement of the sea beneath him as it pushed him ever farther away from his loved ones.

The medical officer grimaced when he came to examine Ramon's wound the following morning.

"It isn't healing as it should, I'll need to stitch it. When we arrive, I recommend you stay on board a few days to give your leg a chance to recover, unless you want to spend the rest of your life limping."

Ramon accepted the offer, war could wait a few more days.

Barcelona was unlike anything Ramon had imagined. Red and black flags of the Communists and the Anarchists hung from buildings along Las Ramblas, the city's wide boulevard running up from the port. Signs outside shops and businesses announced they had been 'collectivised', posters on walls stridently declared 'No pasaran', they shall not pass, and loud speakers played revolutionary music.

There was none of Seville's sartorial elegance on display. The population had adopted overalls and similarly drab outfits. Churches looked as if they'd been bombed, which clearly they hadn't since the other buildings around them showed no signs of being burned or missing masonry.

Asking a man for directions to where he should go to join the army, Ramon was rebuked.

"Señor-"

'I'm comrade, not señor. We are all comrades now."
Impressed that the workers had taken over and
that everyone seemed cheerful and enthusiastic,
Ramon would discover the disadvantage of the
free for all was a constant infighting between
the various factions. The writ of the central
government in Madrid was weak here by the
Mediterranean.

Christmas 1936 in Seville was a sombre affair
for a great number of the inhabitants, so many
empty chairs at family gatherings. For Beatriz, it
would be a brother lost and the father of her child
gone; for Carmelita, a mother lost and a brother
gone. The familial certainties that made a difficult
life bearable were broken. The only certainty was
uncertainty.

Beatriz retrieved the family nativity set from
the back of the cupboard, carefully positioning
each piece on the table. The familiarity of the
figures was comforting. Their paintwork might
be chipped and faded but they brought back
memories of childhood excitement and laughter.
Christmas trees weren't a Spanish tradition but
nearly every family possessed a nativity set.

Her mother took to her bed on the afternoon of
Christmas Eve and wouldn't reappear until the day
after Christmas, sending her daughter away each
time Beatriz went to check on her.

"She seems almost to have lost the will to live,"

confided Beatriz in Carmelita.

"Next year will be different. She'll have a grandchild to dote on. Imagine, Beatriz, next Christmas, a baby. What a wonderful thing that will be."

Beatriz rubbed her protruding tummy in a circular motion. "Yes, you're right, it will be."

"And maybe this horrid war will be over and Ramon will be back."

"I hope so." Beatriz feigned a smile. She wanted to believe it but didn't. She couldn't see how the hatred she'd witnessed would end just because the Nationalists won as many said they were going to, and often she struggled to believe Ramon could still be alive.

"Is something wrong?" asked Carmelita, noticing the doleful, faraway look in Beatriz's eyes.

"No, nothing. The baby's moving about, did you want to feel it kick?" She placed Carmelita's hand on her stomach. "There, that's one."

Carmelita's face shone. "That's incredible. I'm so grateful, Beatriz, that you took me in. I owe you so much."

"Not at all, you are working and taking care of us. And it's like having a sister again. I had two, younger than me. Neither reached their fifth birthday. You have filled the hole they left."

They didn't go to mass at midnight as in previous years both of them always had. The Church supported Queipo and Franco, whose men had murdered their loved ones. Instead, they saw in the day in the flickering candlelit shadow of the room.

CHAPTER 19

Ramon spent a grim Christmas under low leaden skies in mountainous terrain. At the Lenin barracks in Barcelona the training had been rudimentary, even worse than he'd received in Seville when conscripted into the Legion. They practiced without rifles because there weren't enough to go around. Those the Republicans possessed were needed for soldiers fighting at the front.

The main difference Ramon noticed was discipline. There was a lack of it in Barcelona. Individuals ignored orders or argued about them without consequences. Ramon, having experienced the iron fist discipline of Franco's army, began to doubt the ability of the Republicans to win the war.

Transferred to the front in early December, his column had to march over a hundred kilometres in rain and hail, ascending and descending in endless succession the crinkled topography of Europe's most mountainous country after Switzerland.

How Ramon yearned for the kiss of Andalusia's

sun which shone nearly every day of the year. In retrospect, his trek in high summer through Extremadura and Portugal's Alentejo had been easy by comparison. Villages here in the North weren't the whitewashed smile of the South but the scowl of grey stone as unwelcoming in appearance as the wet, scree-covered hillsides they were rooted to.

Frequently the men were forced to wade across fast flowing rivers, holding their kit above their heads. They stumbled in the cold water which could knock a man down if it came above the knee. Ramon saw several swept away, tossed about like logs, their arms flailing in the rapids lower down. The lucky ones reappeared, shivering and bleeding after being smashed against rocks.

The front wasn't a conventional one. The two armies were separated by a steep valley and had positioned themselves too far apart to shoot. It seemed neither side possessed the appetite to fight during these dismal months.

The state of the trenches wasn't much better than the prison ship in which Ramon had been interned in Seville. Rats scurried around day and night and the stink of excrement was ever present.

The Republican government's entreaties to the western powers that Germany and Italy were flouting the non-intervention agreement fell on deaf ears. With Russia the only significant supplier of arms to the Republicans, the Soviets were able to exert considerable influence and pressurise the government in Madrid to move further to the left. Although Stalin's support was far from whole hearted. More than a Francoist Spain, he feared a Communist one might drive Britain and France into an alliance with Germany against the Soviet Union.

That winter, Izil found himself based in Salamanca, which was serving as the Nationalist's temporary capital. In the Plaza Mayor, the grand central square, enclosed by fine baroque architecture of sandstone, he was seated at a pavement cafe with another member of La Guardia Mora drinking coffee beneath a cloudless, cerulean January sky.

Although it was only three in the afternoon the sun had already sunk low, accentuating the contrast between areas bathed in sunlight and those out of it. The men shifted their chairs to escape the lengthening fingers of shadow. This also had the advantage that they were closer to two señoritas at a nearby table who had been giving them coquettish glances.

Izil's Spanish was by now almost fluent. Encouraged by their interest, he and his companion engaged them in conversation and spiked their curiosity.

"Are you in the army?" asked the one who'd caught Izil's attention with her impish face and curly black hair which fell to her shoulders.

"We are members of La Guardia Mora, bodyguards

to El Caudillo."

"El Caudillo," both young women repeated in a reverent tone, wide-eyed and unable to conceal how impressed they were.

By the end of their conversation, Izil had arranged to meet Maria the following day. He returned to the barracks a happy man. Despite the camaraderie amongst the guards, Izil often experienced a surge of emptiness, a profound loneliness enveloping him like low clouds obscuring his mountain home. His plan to visit his family last year had come to nothing when he was transferred to Spain and he missed them. Maria was the spark of joy he sorely needed.

They met often after their first date but never in such public places as Plaza Mayor. Izil understood Maria's reasons. Franco might speak of a Hispanic-Moroccan brotherhood, but to Spaniards on both sides of the conflict Moroccans were a reminder of Al-Andalus. They weren't and never could be their brothers, and the disapproving looks would have been universal.

Maria's lips were a delicious distraction, dispelling his homesickness. At night, Izil lay thinking of her and what might happen when the war ended. She'd already told him how she would love to see Morocco, and Izil was no longer a pauper. In time, his accumulated earnings should be more than needed to support a wife and family, enough to buy a house in Tetouan and start his own business.

Carmelita woke each day with knots in her stomach, wondering if today might be the day when Francisco would be at home. Approaching the oversized front door, she drew the corner of her black headscarf across her mouth, ready to run should he open the door.

While she cleaned, she listened. The tap of the doorknob would cause Carmelita to run and hide in a nearby room or rush out onto the patio and seek refuge amongst the large plants, her heart in her mouth. Greetings from another female voice would sound the all clear. A masculine one, which was rare, would leave Carmelita in place until she had determined it wasn't him. Gradually she became less fearful, the man never once made it home before she finished and left for siesta.

The morning Carmelita saw the Doña crying in the lounge through a half open door, she tried to tiptoe past but her mop hit the side of the metal bucket she was carrying. The clank was loud and the Doña looked up from her chair, her eyes red.

Carmelita felt compelled to enquire. "Are you all right?"

"No, and I never will be." Carmelita didn't know how to respond, to ask for details would be prying. The Doña volunteered them. "They say God works in mysterious ways, and I for one will never understand his reasons. The doctors say I'm barren, that I'll never have children."

"I'm sorry."

"It's absurd, isn't it? Me, rich and able to provide a child a good home. And you, you'd probably fall pregnant the moment you tried, but no one will want to try with you. How can anyone make sense of this life?" Carmelita didn't know what to say. The Doña threw out a hand to dismiss her. "Carry on with your work, and don't breathe a word of this to anyone." There was a sharpness in her tone now, an anger at herself for sharing her secret with a mere maid.

Carmelita nodded submissively. Later, down on her knees while she scrubbed the patio tiles, her own tears flowed. The woman was right, Carmelita would never have a baby of her own. No man would ever want to touch her, let alone love her.

CHAPTER 20

His commander's face when he entered the dormitory was severe but in a way which conveyed sympathy rather than annoyance. Izil's father had died and Izil was given permission to make a brief visit home. After travelling, he would have only one night to spend with his family.

This time Izil didn't make the long walk up into the mountains. He hired a donkey. Climbing into the windswept, rock strewn landscape cemented his plans to live in the more welcoming climate of Tetouan when he finally returned.

On arrival, he embraced his mother and sister. They were as thin as twigs and their faces drawn. Tafrara, his sister, had lost that carefree sparkle of childhood.

"Where's Idir?"

"Your brother's gone searching for a job in Tetouan. We've nothing left. The goats died and we're almost out of food," answered Izil's mother.

Izil sighed. "If only father hadn't refused the money I tried to send, he could have had the treatment he needed and you would all have had full stomachs."

"He was a proud man, and a stubborn one."

"You must take this." Izil handed over the little goatskin bag bulging with banknotes. "There's enough to no longer have to worry and you'll be able to buy new goats. I'll send more. When you hear from Idir, you can call him back. I've also brought food."

That evening they feasted, the soft glow of firelight revealing beaming faces. Happiness, too long absent from their mountain home, had returned.

"I wish I could have seen father one more time and told him of how I fought in a holy war against those who deny the existence of Allah, and how I am now in an elite guard to protect the Spanish leader. Let me show you a photograph."

His mother briefly examined the picture he produced from the inside pocket of his jacket but passed no comment and promptly handed it back

"Aren't you proud of your son?"

"I want my son back home."

"I'll return as soon as I can."

"And when will that be?"

"I can't say."

Izil could sense his mother had something on her mind she wasn't sharing. "What are you thinking?"

"Why do they dress you up like that?"

"Dress up? Don't you think I look magnificent? You should see the surprise on the Spaniards' faces the first time they see us. The Moors they so looked down upon, now so grand and majestic."

"Or are they just using you as part of their game, as delusional fools." Izil bit his tongue, he had less than twenty four hours and didn't want an argument. "You should come home and take a wife."

"I'll come home when I can, and maybe with a wife."

His mother's face wrinkled in concern. "What kind of wife? Not an infidel, I hope."

"She would convert."

"And have you discussed this with her?"

"Not exactly but I'm sure she'll agree when I propose. We'll come and live in Tetouan. I'll have enough money to buy a house and start a business, and you can all come live with us."

"Your father would have wanted you to marry a nice Muslim girl."

"I'm head of the family now and will do as I wish," said Izil tersely. "Let's not spoil this lovely evening," he added, noticing the hurt on his mother's face.

Pondering the days' events while he lay waiting for an elusive sleep to come, Izil felt flat. Things weren't as he thought they would be. He had certainly changed, he no longer belonged in these mountains of his birth.

Arriving back in Salamanca, Izil was looking forward to seeing Maria again. Told to report to the commander's office, he wondered why.

"How was your trip home?"

"Good, sir."

"I've had a complaint."

"Complaint?"

"Yes, it seems you're seeing a young woman. Her father objects and asks that you stay away from her."

"Has anyone asked her what she wants?" countered Izil.

The commander's voice hardened. "That's not the issue. We are fighting to restore traditional values, the values of church and family. I'm sure you understand, after all the same values of faith and family apply to Islam. You need to choose, La Guardia Mora or the girl. If you choose the girl, you'll be back at the front with the Regulares. You will fall in love again, but the honour of being in La Guardia is a once in a lifetime opportunity." He raised his hand to silence Izil's attempt to protest. "Give me your answer in the morning. Dismissed."

Izil's shoulders slumped as he made his way across the courtyard of the barracks. He was beginning to realise the price he would have to pay for success. He wouldn't really belong in his own world or his new one but be obliged to live in the cracks in between, accepted by no one for who he had become.

It was an April afternoon, one when the Feria d'Abril would normally have been in full swing, and when the optimism it brought would have energised Seville and made it the best place to be in all of Europe. This year the festival had been cancelled by the authorities. Those who had suffered so since the coup didn't care. Their loss was still much too raw to contemplate partying.

When Carmelita arrived back from her morning's work, Beatriz had her arms outstretched and both hands pressed against the uneven, stone wall of the downstairs room for support.

"It's time," said her mother.

Beatriz groaned in pain.

"What can I do?" volunteered Carmelita.

"Precious little. I can't imagine you know anything about childbirth. You haven't had four of them like I have. I suggest you leave and don't come back until tomorrow. You'll only be in the way."

"No, I want her here," insisted Beatriz. "Carmelita, you can hold my hand."

At times, Carmelita thought Beatriz might break the bones in her hand so tightly did she squeeze when the contractions intensified. It wasn't until dawn that Ramona was born. Carmelita was convinced the child must be stillborn, her skin had such an unexpected deathly pallor. Beatriz's mother cut the umbilical cord and held the girl by her feet and thwacked her bottom, producing crying and a rush of colour to her body. After washing her in a bowl, the woman handed the baby wrapped in a small blanket to her daughter who lay exhausted on the bed but her eyes were glowing.

Her face expressionless as a stone, Beatriz's mother showed no joy. "You should seriously consider giving her away. It would be for the best. Your so-called husband, if that's what he is, won't be coming back, and no man wants to take on another's child. You've seen how few men are left in Triana, but you have the beauty to catch one if you put your mind to it."

"I won't give my daughter away, never."

"In that case, you'll die an old maid like Carmelita will. I only want what's best for you but clearly I'm wasting my breath. I'm going out for some fresh air." The woman slammed the door.

"I can't believe she's my mother sometimes."

"I wish Ramona could have known her other grandmother," said Carmelita.

"Me too. And ignore that nonsense about Ramon not coming back. He will, just as soon as this war is over." Beatriz doubted her own words but didn't want to share that with Carmelita. "Do you think she looks like him?"

Carmelita gazed at the small, squashed nose and closed eyes. "It's hard to say right now but I'm sure she will when she grows. What a little angel she is, absolute perfection."

CHAPTER 21

Beatriz and Carmelita found their sunshine in Ramona, an affirmation that tomorrow would be better. They learned to ignore the deep sighs and sullen looks of Beatriz's mother.

"She can wallow in misery if she wants," commented Beatriz when her mother went off to the market, "but I will not be sucked into it."

"She's very different to you," said Carmelita.

"I would hope so. She changed after my sisters died. She withdrew into herself, and even more so when my father and brother were murdered. It hasn't been easy for her but she's not the only one to suffer."

"Maybe I'm part of the problem and should move out."

"Absolutely not, I love your company. I'd go insane stuck with her on my own, if you can put up with her that is."

"I'm used to how people treat me so don't worry about that."

A couple of months after the birth, Beatriz began practising flamenco once more. In October, she entered a competition in Seville which she won. Soon she found herself in high demand across the city. To her surprise, flamenco moved out of the shadows. Its association with the gitano community no longer condemned it to the backstreets. Franco commandeered it to suit his own agenda. He decided it could take its place alongside bullfighting as something quintessentially Spanish and become a cultural bedrock of traditional values.

Under his rule, flamenco would spread all over Spain and no longer be limited to Andalusia, even if some of the practices elsewhere, such as the use of castanets, had little to do with genuine flamenco. In time, barely any travel poster for Spain would be without either a bullfighter or a flamenco dancer.

From the money Beatriz was earning and that which Carmelita was contributing, Beatriz began putting some aside for Carmelita's operation. She sowed a pocket inside one of her flamenco dresses to hide it and hung the dress back in the cupboard. When Beatriz had saved enough, she would surprise the woman she now thought of as a sister. Beatriz liked to imagine the moment. She would ask Carmelita to get the dress out of the cupboard and tell her to look inside. It made her smile to think of Carmelita's reaction when she found out what the bundle of notes were intended for.

That thought and Ramona were the bright side of Beatriz's life but her other hopes remained in darkness, unfulfilled. The war ground on month after month and the Nationalists were conquering ever more of the country. There was no way of knowing if Ramon was alive and whether he'd ever be able to return if he was. Beatriz was grateful she had flamenco. She could lose herself in her dancing when fear about the future and the ache in her heart for Ramon threatened to bring her down.

By the beginning of 1939, the Republican army was falling back towards Barcelona and daily air raids were pulverising the city.

Ramon had grown a thick beard. It hid a face wound acquired during a failed attempt to push back Franco's men from the coast and regain lost territory which had split the Republican zone into two. Yet Ramon's eyes couldn't hide the scars of his mind after nearly a thousand days of death and destruction. He'd witnessed too much brutality. He tried not to think about it, but even when he succeeded his dreams brought it all back. Most mornings, Ramon awoke sweating and traumatised after a night of reliving it once more.

The Republican government desperately tried to hang on in the belief that if Hitler started a war, France and Britain would finally help them in the struggle against Hitler's friend, Franco. But time was fast running out.

Towards the end of January, news reached the city that Franco's forces were crossing the Rio

Llobregat to the south of Barcelona. Panic spread through the population as quickly as a tinder-dry summer's fire. That the Nationalists executed those who might have any connection with their opponents, however tenuous, was common knowledge. Thick smoke rose from the chimneys of government ministries and the offices of trade unions while those inside frantically burned papers that would implicate them.

Civilians and soldiers began moving out of the city in whatever way they could, a fortunate few in vehicles or on horse and cart but most on foot, bringing with them only those possessions they could carry. Ramon joined the exodus.

When he passed the hospital, the wounded who could move had already crawled from their hospital beds and now sat or lay by the roadside. Those still with arms stretched them out in supplication. "Help us, please. Take us with you. "

Their pleas were desperate. Everybody knew injuries would be seen by the attackers as a sure sign of having fought against them. Franco's men had already shot the wounded found in hospitals in other cities they had captured.

Nearly all those passing the wounded ignored their pitiful pleas and stared resolutely ahead. Ramon's conscience was pricked. He had killed a fellow Republican to save himself, it was time to do something good. He bent down next to a man with a bandage over one eye and both his legs missing below the knee. Taking the man by the arms,

Ramon hauled him onto his back and staggered forwards under the weight.

It was over a hundred and fifty kilometres to the French border and France had closed it, but the sorry column of half a million refugees moved towards it. They had nowhere else to go.

Despite the bitter cold, those fleeing welcomed the frequent rain and sleet. Low clouds grounded Franco's aircraft. Breaks in the weather brought that horrible drone, demons diving from the sky, strafing, bombing. Possessions were abandoned in the dash away from the road. Bodies were left where they fell. Dark brought peace but many young and old died from exhaustion and exposure, not waking after another night out in the open.

A constant pain made its home in Ramon's back. He was having to put the man he carried down on the ground every couple of hundred metres. Ramon asked others if they could help and take turns. He received only shaking heads or blank stares of rebuke that he should ask such a thing when they could barely manage to carry on themselves.

They passed through a village and Ramon took his human cargo from house to house. Some greeted him with the end of a rifle. All refused to help. All except one, a woman living on her own.

"I'll take him. They killed my son. God must have sent me your friend to take care of instead."

At last, the long column of refugees approached the frontier with France. Word came down the line from the thousands ahead of Ramon. The trek had been in vain. The border remained shut.

CHAPTER 22

Izil's decision to remain in the Moorish Guard cost him the chance of love. He persuaded himself that even if Maria had accepted his proposal and he survived the war as a front line soldier, she wouldn't have coped with a life in Morocco, a life away from her family and culture.

Izil found solace in his horse, a beautiful creature with long eyelashes and attractive dark eyes. Izil named him Tariq after Tariq ibn Ziyad, who had led his Berber army from North Africa to conquer Spain. It was a name Izil shared only with other Moroccans. Tariq wasn't a name that would be appreciated by Spaniards.

Izil and Tariq travelled throughout Spain's Nationalist zone, which encompassed most of the country, their itinerary dictated by wherever El Caudillo wished to impress the local population. On days off, Izil and his fellow guards rode out into the countryside. They never ceased to get a thrill from observing villagers' open-mouthed disbelief at witnessing Moors confidently trotting three abreast through the tumbledown streets of dust and looking like sultans, more magnificent than anyone the inhabitants had ever set eyes upon.

On one occasion, a member of the Civil Guard waved them down with his pistol, demanding to know who they were. Producing their papers, they left the man red faced for having challenged members of Franco's own guard.

Barcelona fell and Franco held a victory parade. La Guardia Mora took part. After the parade in Barcelona, Izil brushed Tariq in the barrack stables while he thought of the day, of the pro Franco residents of the city who, no longer obliged to hide their allegiance, had come out to cheer the troops. They'd cheered the Regulares too. He wondered for how long Franco's supporters would be cheering Moroccans once the war ended. An end which couldn't be many months away. With Barcelona taken, the capture of Madrid was bound to follow. Once the Nationalists were victorious they would no longer have any use for Izil and his fellow countrymen. Thousands of Moroccan soldiers on Spanish soil would then be seen as a threat.

Carmelita had been working at the house in Calle de Placentines for over two years. It was a good job. The Doña paid her on time and left her to get on with things, rarely directing her or engaging in conversation which suited Carmelita. However, today the Doña had specific instructions.

"I'd like you to do the patio first. My husband will be home for lunch and we shall be eating outside.

I really must introduce you to Don Francisco, it's about time he met you." She eyed Carmelita quizzically. "Is something the matter?"

"No, I'm just feeling a little dizzy."

"You should drink a glass of water before you start."

Carmelita's heart beat like a drum while she scrubbed the patio. She'd almost forgotten, forgotten that he lived in this house. Carmelita cleaned as fast as she could. Shortly before one she approached the Doña.

"I'm sorry but I'm feeling unwell. I've finished the cleaning, would you mind if I left?"

"That's a shame. It would have been nice for you to meet my husband, but I don't want you passing on whatever it is you have. Stay away until you're better."

Carmelita pulled open the heavy door. She was about to turn left and go down the street towards La Giralda like she always did when she spotted the man coming towards her, only metres away. Carmelita pulled her headscarf across her mouth and walked quickly in the other direction, her legs weak and unsteady. It had been a close encounter, too close. She was playing with fire. It was time she started looking for another job.

Carmelita sighed with relief when she reached the sanctuary of home. Already a toddler, Ramona shouted with glee and ran into Carmelita's arms. Carmelita adored her and cherished such moments. She might never be a mother herself but she was grateful she got to live with her niece and be a part of her life. Beatriz's mother ignored the child except when scolding her. It would be Carmelita who would take care of Ramona for the rest of the day to allow Beatriz to rest and get ready for her evening shows.

The owner of the club approached Beatriz at the end of her late show. The club was a small, intimate venue in Santa Cruz where the foot stamping and clapping bounced off the walls and the tables around which customers sat were jammed closely together.

"That man over there by the table at the back would like you to join him for a drink."

"I don't join men for a drink," retorted Beatriz sharply.

"I recommend you don't ignore this one. He's powerful, deputy to the Governor. One word from him and you could find it difficult to dance in any of the city's top venues again."

Beatriz peered across the room. In the subdued lighting and fog of cigarette smoke it was difficult to see clearly, but she could make out the outline of his face looking in her direction.

Picking up the train of her dress, she squeezed her way past the other tables. The man leapt up and pulled a chair out for her, bowing slightly in greeting.

"Encantado. Please, sit. What would you like to drink?"

"An amontillado."

"An excellent choice." He clicked his fingers to attract the waiter's attention.

Beatriz examined the man. He had an aristocratic air, an aquiline nose and thin pencil moustache. His black hair was greased back and there was a cloying smell about him, the result of eau de cologne too liberally applied. His suit, white shirt, and red and yellow striped tie, mimicking the colours of the Spanish flag, were all premium quality.

"You are a splendid dancer, Beatriz."

"How do you know my name?"

"The owner told me." The waiter arrived with her drink. The man raised his glass. "Salud."

Beatriz wet her lips with a sip.

"How long have you danced?"

"All my life, except when I was pregnant with my daughter."

"How old is she?"

"Nearly two."

"And what does your husband do?"

Beatriz balked. "Is this an interrogation?"

"No, but what you don't tell me I have ways of finding out." Beatriz detected a hint of menace before he quickly softened his tone. "I've enjoyed watching you dance. Maybe I can do something for you."

"And what would you want in return?"

"Is that how little you think of me? That I would only help you if you made it worth my while?"

It was precisely what Beatriz thought. She decided to ask, however. She hated not knowing.

"There is something you could do for me."

"Name it."

"My husband left-"

"You mean he was a Republican."

"No, but I was afraid what might happen to him in the confusion of war so I persuaded him to go away, and I don't know where he is."

"I could certainly help. If he has become a prisoner of war, there'll be records, and if the worst has happened at least you'll know one way or the other. What's his name?"

"Ramon. Ramon Garcia."

"I'll make enquiries. Come to my office in the Town Hall at noon two weeks from today. Ask for me, Francisco Castillo Morales, and tell the guards that I've summoned you. It's been a pleasure talking to you, Beatriz, but I should leave and let you get home to your daughter."

CHAPTER 23

Three days had passed. In the coughing and clearing of throats on a morose grey dusk, Ramon heard talk that some had gone farther inland to take their chances crossing the Pyrenees.

Ramon considered his options. The French couldn't patrol all the high passes, especially in the middle of winter, and it wouldn't be long before Franco's troops advanced to the border. The risk of dying in an attempt to cross the mountains had to be better than doing nothing and waiting to be massacred. Ramon decided to leave first thing in the morning. There could be a chance of food too, perhaps somebody in one of the mountain villages would take pity on him and throw him a crust. Here there was nothing to eat.

At first light Ramon wandered off, soon leaving the road behind him. A hard frost crunched underfoot and the mountain peaks on the horizon covered in thick snow looked deceptively alluring in the early morning sunlight which shone on them with such brilliance. Turning as he crested the first hill, Ramon was astonished to see below him the long column of refugees up and moving forwards. He ran down the hill and across the fields.

"What's happening?" he asked an old man shuffling along at the rear.

"The French have relented, they're letting us in," he said exposing an almost toothless grin.

At the border, the women and children were separated from the men and Ramon's rifle and bandolier were confiscated. The men were told to walk behind a truck. They marched all day and through the night and come morning were by the coast. A long sandy beach ran as far as the eye could see. Ordered to stop, Senegalese soldiers with skin the colour of mahogany directed the men onto the sand and into a large enclosure delineated by rolls of barbed wire. Ramon's heart sank. He'd reached France but here freedom was also to be denied.

The soldiers tossed baguettes over the wire and laughed at the consequences. The men fell upon them, pulling them apart as they each fought for a share and quickly shoved whatever they'd managed to grab into their mouths before another tried to take it from them.

A stormy sea of pewter and white spume crashed onto the beach, and a howling wind threw spray into the air. The salt stung Ramon's eyes and rubbing them with his fingers only made it worse.

He joined a group digging down into the sand with their bare hands to create a hollow for shelter. Soon the sand was wet to the touch, but it was preferable to a night of being sandblasted in a wind which took the air temperature below freezing. How Ramon yearned once more for the life affirming climate of Andalusia where even in winter it was rarely cold.

The conditions they faced were primitive. There was a complete absence of washing facilities or toilets. The sea had to serve for both.

Ramon was woken by an unfamiliar sound, soft yet unsettling. An avalanche of sand collapsed into the hollow. Ramon leapt out of its way but the man asleep next to him disappeared under it. Most of the dugout had been filled, and with it the men sheltering there.

In the sepulchral light cast by a full moon moving out from behind clouds, survivors clawed at the sand. The first man unearthed wore round spectacles, now cracked, his face white as a phantom's. Unlike others he was dressed in a suit,.

"He's dead," pronounced one of the rescuers.

Ramon kneeled and placed his fingers in the man's mouth. He removed sand and began mouth to mouth and repeated compressions on his chest, something he had learned at the front. The man coughed, vomiting up more sand and breathed. Ramon returned to digging. None of the others who had been entombed came out alive.

Later that morning while Ramon sat staring out to sea wondering how much longer he would survive here, exposed to the elements night and day, the man approached him still wearing his cracked glasses.

"They told me what you did. You saved my life. How can I repay you?"

"By getting me out of here," replied Ramon flippantly.

"I will try."

"Good luck with that." Ramon went back to looking out to sea.

Not long afterwards, the man returned. "Come with me, we're leaving."

"That's not even funny."

"I don't have time to debate."

Ramon stood up. "You're not joking then?"

"Why would I? I was a Minister in the government. I was able to speak to the French officer in charge and get him to confirm my claim. When he said arrangements would be made to get me to Paris to join the government in exile, I told him that I must bring my assistant. Are you coming or not?"

Francisco Castillo Morales glanced at the clock on the wall and tapped his fingers on the desk with irritation. It was already gone noon. He was a man who got what he wanted. She might be a prickly character but he enjoyed a challenge. Her charisma had captivated him.

He picked up the photograph lying on his desk. He'd remembered the man when he saw his face, looking sombre in his Legionnaires' uniform. Ramon Garcia, that peasant from the village who should have faced a firing squad, only saved because of who his mistress had been. The rat had deserted and never been caught. Hopefully, he was six feet under by now like all traitors deserved to be.

Beatriz approached the Ayuntamiento, the Town Hall, in Plaza San Francisco. Its exterior stone carving, intricate and stunning, created a soft and inviting facade, but this belied its inner workings. Beatriz's stomach rumbled, she was nervous about visiting the lair of those governing this city, those who had murdered her father and brother, and nervous as to what she might find out about Ramon. Beatriz feared today would be the day she discovered the father of her daughter was dead.

A guard directed her to the second floor. Francisco rose from his chair and came across the room to greet her with a smile she found insincere and calculating. He shut the door behind her.

"You came. I was beginning to think you wouldn't. Do sit. Can I offer you a sherry - amontillado, isn't it?"

"No thank you. I never drink during the day."

Beatriz took in her surroundings. His office was large with a view over the square below. Light streaming in highlighted dust motes swirling in the air. On the wall behind his desk hung a large sepia photograph of Franco, emperor like in an overcoat with an extravagantly wide fur collar draped on his shoulders and over his uniform.

Francisco offered her a cigarette which she declined. He proceeded to light one for himself, sat down and leaned back in his green leather chair, exhaling and blowing smoke rings in a display of power.

"We have tracked down Ramon," he remarked in a casual manner. "You'll be glad to know he's alive."

"Really?" Beatriz sat up even straighter. Inside she experienced an explosion of joy. "Is he well?"

"Very, he is a valued soldier in the Legion."

"The Legion?"

"You seem surprised. Was he a traitor?"

"No, it's just... he didn't mention he was going to sign up."

"Well, he did. Would you like to see a photograph?" Francisco handed her the picture.

Beatriz knew instantly it was Ramon. "Do you know where he is?"

"With his fellow patriots, surrounding Madrid in the final push for victory."

"Thank you for finding out for me. It's wonderful news to know he may soon get to meet his daughter." Beatriz forced a smile and stood up to go not wanting to remain a moment longer.

"There's no need to rush off." Francisco stood and approached her. "I do have some other information about him which I feel duty bound to share with you. Ramon has met somebody else, they've been together for a couple of years. She lives in Toledo. He always spends his leave there, with her." Beatriz failed to mask her disappointment at this second blow. Francisco placed a hand on her arm. "I'm sorry he's let you

THE SHADOWS OF SEVILLE

down. You owe him nothing, he's not worthy of you. You're a precious jewel, a jewel who should be worshipped, who should have whatever her heart desires."

Beatriz became rigid. Francisco took hold of her other arm and pulled her to him, planting his mouth roughly on hers. Beatriz tried to move away but he wouldn't release her. He pushed her backwards onto the desk and shoved a hand up her dress, his breathing heavy, his eyes wild and determined. She struggled but he was too strong. "Don't fight it, you know you want it," he insisted.

"Stop!" But he didn't. Raising the arm he'd temporarily let go of, Beatriz reached out for his face only centimetres from hers. Digging her nails in as hard as she could, she pulled them swiftly down his face.

"Aargh!" Francisco shot up sharply, placing his hand on his cheek as if that would end the pain. Beatriz ran for the door. "You gitana whore! You'll pay for this."

"Try anything and I'll tell your wife," shot back Beatriz before racing down the stairs and out of the building.

Francisco went to look in the gilded mirror on the wall opposite his desk. Four long lines, red with blood, were engraved on his skin from the corner of his left eye to his chin. His most immediate concern was how he was going to explain that to Luisa, his wife.

Beatriz hurried through back streets blinking back

tears, tears for having been assaulted but most of all tears for what she now knew about Ramon.

CHAPTER 24

Ramon pushed open the small window in the attic where he slept and poked his head out for a better view. Here, in Montmartre, he could see Paris laid out below him. The Eiffel Tower standing tall above the rooftops like an iron rocket dominated the city skyline.

Not since before the civil war had Ramon's life been this calm. No longer did he wake each day thinking it could well be his last. He still fretted about Beatriz and his family. He wanted to send them a letter to let them know he was alive and well, but others warned him against it. Correspondence would be intercepted, they said, and would endanger those to whom it was addressed. If the Nationalists couldn't punish those who fought against them, they punished their families instead.

Ramon descended the steep streets on his bicycle. It sent vibrations through his body as it juddered on the cobbles. There was hope in his heart for the first time in a long while. Franco might be on the point of victory, but Luis, the man he'd saved on the beach, had told him a war which would engulf all of Europe was becoming increasingly likely by the day. Finally, Britain and France would be forced to make a stand against Hitler and they would change their policy of neutrality and want to see an end to Franco's regime. Franco would probably join the war on the side of his fellow fascists, Mussolini and Hitler. Britain and France would win, Luis assured him, and Spain would once again be free. Then they could all return and rebuild their ravaged country and rejoin loved ones left behind.

Ramon halted outside a pavement cafe to indulge in his new morning routine. He savoured the rich, dark coffee and the buttery taste of his croissant. It was a privilege to sit and watch the world go by, not to live in constant fear and hunger. Montmartre was an eclectic mix of artists, writers, intellectuals, and bohemian characters. Political discourse was lively and often abrasive, but without resorting to killing someone for what they believed in. Ramon fondly imagined how wonderful Spain could become if the predictions of Luis came true. To have the liberty of the French combined with the sunshine and brilliant colours of Andalusia would be a perfect combination.

After using his fingers to mop up the last crumbs from his plate, Ramon got back on his bike and weaved through the morning traffic. He ignored the horns and insults of drivers annoyed by the way he cut in and out, making much faster progress than they could.

Near the centre he reached his destination, an unremarkable building which served as the headquarters of the remnants of the Republican government. Leaving his bike in the corridor, he bounded up the stairs to start his work day. The room he entered was alive with the clatter of typewriters and smelled of cigarette smoke. Lying on a desk, the black silhouette of the dancer on a carton of the popular 'Gitanes' brand, French for gypsies, reminded Ramon of Beatriz.

Ramon greeted his fellow workers. Typists and former government ministers shared the same space. The former at one end of the room, the latter sitting around a large table at the other.

Ramon collected his first batch of deliveries for the day and went back out. When they reached Paris, Luis had secured him a job as the office courier. It hadn't taken Ramon long until he knew how to get to locations all over the city. The French Foreign Ministry, at the Quai d'Orsay, and the embassies of Britain, the Soviet Union, and Mexico, were the places he most often visited.

None of those in exile trusted the post or the telephone. Rumours were rife that many of Franco's spies were in Paris, intent on sabotaging his enemies. Ramon frequently looked behind him while he cycled. Whenever he thought he was being followed, he abruptly turned his handle bars, jumped the kerb, and went down alleyways too narrow for a car.

Beatriz relaxed. Weeks had passed and the expected revenge of Francisco Castillo Morales hadn't materialised. Her threat to inform his wife must have worked, not that Beatriz knew who she was or where they lived.

At first, Beatriz had been almost unable to perform, her nerves so frayed after the attempted rape. Before each show, she would peep from behind the curtain to see if he was among the audience or whether there were others who looked like they might have been sent by him.

Walking home late at night Beatriz glanced over her shoulder every few steps, anxiety pumping through her veins should she see a man behind her. Reaching an alleyway, she would divert down it and wait for him to pass. And pass the men always did, gradually increasing her confidence.

Beatriz was coming to terms with the news about Ramon. The shock at learning he'd joined the enemy and had a new lover was fading. That explained why he hadn't come back to Seville on leave.

Beatriz didn't want to be with someone who fought for those who had murdered her brother and so many of the men in Triana. Maybe if Ramon knew they'd taken his mother, he would see the error of his ways.

However, as far as Beatriz was concerned, it was too late for regrets or apologies. His betrayal was unforgivable and there was no way back for him into her affections. Beatriz might be obliged to smile at the Nationalists who came to her shows and pretend she agreed with their views to protect herself and Ramona, but she wasn't ever going to marry a man who supported Franco's regime.

She didn't speak to Carmelita about any of it. To shatter her image of her brother and cause her pain seemed cruel. One day Beatriz would have to tell her but not yet. Perhaps after the surgery when Carmelita would be feeling better about herself, or maybe Beatriz would wait until Carmelita met someone and fell in love. Beatriz hoped that would soon happen once Carmelita had the operation.

Carmelita was a beautiful woman, a beauty few saw at present, focussing instead on that gaping hole which went up to her nose and covered the width beneath it. She was such a kind and gentle person. Little Ramona loved her as much as Beatriz did, and Beatriz looked forward to the day Carmelita had a child of her own. She would make such an ideal mother.

Tomorrow night, Beatriz was going to ask Carmelita to take the dress with the money in it from the cupboard. What a special evening it was going to be. Beatriz could hardly wait to see the delight on Carmelita's face when she realised all those years of being disdained and ignored would soon be over.

CHAPTER 25

"Is everything all right?" asked Carmelita arriving back from her work the following afternoon. Beatriz's mother was pacing the floor and wringing her hands, her eyes puffy.

"They took Ramona."

The words hit like bullets and the colour drained from Carmelita's face. "Took Ramona? Who?"

"The blue shirts, the Falangists. They burst in when Beatriz was out shopping. They said the children of Republicans are being taken to orphanages so they can be placed with decent families in other parts of Spain who will bring them up to be good Spaniards and true patriots. There was nothing I could do to stop them."

"Where's Beatriz?"

"I don't know. When I told her she screamed at me, said it was my doing, that I never wanted her to have Ramona. She dropped her shopping bag on the floor and went out. I'm frightened she'll do something stupid and get herself killed." Her normally strident voice broke.

Carmelita moved forwards to hug the woman but

she moved away. The two of them passed the hours in an awkward and rarely interrupted silence.

When Beatriz appeared, her mascara smudged and her hair untidy as if she'd been tugging at it in despair, she collapsed into Carmelita's arms, sobbing.

"My baby, they've taken my baby. I've been to the orphanages but the nuns refuse to let me in and tell me they have no one by that name. They're probably lying but what can I do? I feel so helpless. My little girl must be so afraid, all alone and not understanding why she's been taken from her Mama. The people who do this are monsters."

Carmelita wept with her.

In Madrid, Izil was again part of a victory parade, this time to mark the end of the war. Over one hundred thousand troops took part, including Mussolini's black shirts and Hitler's soldiers. Hundreds of aircraft flew in formation above, blocking the sun. The shadow they created proclaiming the end of democracy in Spain.

On the huge arch behind the reviewing stand the word 'Franco' was emblazoned six times. The man's diatribe was no less venomous in victory than in war:

"Let us not deceive ourselves: the Jewish spirit, which permitted the alliance of big capital with Marxism and which was behind so many pacts with the anti-Spanish revolution cannot be extirpated in one day."

The war had ended the previous month but the killing continued. Those who fought for the losing side or who were accused of having done so were executed and, if not, sentenced to long prison terms.

After the parade, Izil spotted Brahim in a crowd of Regulares. Going over to him, he slapped Brahim on the back.

"My dear friend, praise Allah that you survived." The two men embraced.

"Yes, I was lucky, so many of us didn't. As you know, they always sent us out in front, not caring that we bore the brunt of the casualties. And you, my friend, how is life amongst the elite?"

"It's been mostly good. What will you do now the war is over?"

"I've heard we're soon to be shipped back to Morocco. They've got what they want from us and no longer have to pretend they like or respect us. Still I don't mind, there's nowhere like home. Some of the men have been talking about liberating our own country. I want to be part of that. And what about you, will they let you stay?"

"For now. Franco is vain, he likes the pomp and ceremony we bring. But I don't know for how long. As you say, they only needed us to win their war. At some point, Franco will face criticism that in a Spain he intends to make more fervently Catholic than at any time since they drove our ancestors out of Al-Andalus, he chooses to have Muslims as bodyguards. I'd like to stay while I can, the pay is good."

"Well, don't leave it too long before you come back and join your brothers. Don't become their lackey. I must go now. I hope to see you in Tetouan before long, Inshallah."

Izil rejoined his fellow guards and rode to the vast El Pardo palace outside Madrid. Now Franco's home, it was also where La Guardia Mora had their barracks.

Carmelita walked to work with a heavy heart. It was nearly dawn before they'd fallen asleep. Carmelita had crept out, hoping to allow Beatriz a little more rest until she awoke to the torment that would now plague her every waking moment.

Doña Luisa opened the door looking more radiant than Carmelita had ever seen her. Normally her greeting would be limited to 'buenos dias' but not today.

"God has granted me my wish. A child!"

"Congratulations," said Carmelita, mustering what little enthusiasm she could in response to the news of her boss's pregnancy.

"She's in the room next to ours, sleeping."

"I don't understand."

"I'm not expecting if that's what you thought. Francisco has brought me a beautiful girl from the orphanage. A child who wasn't wanted by her own parents. We will give her the love and care she deserves. Don't go in there, and be careful not to disturb her while you're working."

Carmelita began her work downstairs. When she went upstairs, Carmelita walked across the tiles as quietly as she could. She placed her head against the closed door to the girl's room. There was no sound. Carmelita set about cleaning the owners' bedroom.

She stopped, noise was coming from the next room. Unable to resist her curiosity, Carmelita went back out into the corridor. The child wasn't making a lot of noise but sounded distressed. Carmelita pushed down on the door handle. The shutters were closed and the room in shadow but she could make out a girl of about two years of age standing up in a cot.

The girl smiled through her tears. "Carmi."

Astonished, Carmelita rushed over and hugged her niece.

"Where's Mama? I want to go home."

"You will, I'll take you but you need to be very quiet. Can you do that for me?" whispered Carmelita.

Ramona nodded with solemnity.

Carmelita lifted Ramona into her arms, a bundle of warmth and softness smelling of soap scented with lemons. Content, the little girl rested her head on Carmelita's shoulder and sucked her thumb. Carmelita's mind was whirring. She was terrified but if she could only get Ramona out of here and back to Triana they could all leave and go somewhere no one would find them.

Carmelita crept down the stairs step by step,

holding her precious cargo tightly. Up ahead, she could see that large door, the final barrier. A ray of bright light penetrated the division between the two halves as if the kingdom of heaven was beyond it, beckoning her.

Carmelita halted and listened. All was quiet. She made for the door and began to pull it open. Carmelita experienced an adrenaline rush of triumph, she was going to make it.

"What do you think you're doing!" She recognised the rasping voice. Francisco appeared and blocked their escape. Behind her, Carmelita heard the click of heels.

"What's happening?" asked Luisa.

Ramona screamed and flailed as Francisco prised her from Carmelita's arms. "Take her up to her room," he commanded Luisa.

Francisco produced a handgun from the holster on his waist hidden by his jacket. He angrily shoved Carmelita. "Get in there! Sit." From his office, he telephoned the police. "It's Francisco Castillo Morales. I need you to come to my home immediately. I've just apprehended the maid trying to kidnap our child." Slamming the phone down, he glared at Carmelita. Like a bull working up to a charge, he circled her.

"Why were you stealing our daughter?" Receiving no answer, he struck her hard across the face. Carmelita's head jerked sideways from the impact. "Wait a minute, don't I know you? You look familiar."

"I don't think so. There are many others in Seville with my affliction."

He brought his face close to hers. His breath reeked of garlic and his eyes were crazy like those of a rabid dog. "Where were you taking Carmen?" he snarled.

Carmelita was thinking quickly, desperately trying to come up with an explanation. She didn't want Beatriz to be caught up in this. "I...I've always wanted a baby of my own. When I saw her I couldn't help myself."

"You're disgusting. I should have shot you dead but that would have frightened little Carmen. No matter, you can rot in jail instead."

Within minutes, two members of La Guardia Civil arrived. They led Carmelita away. By evening she had been thrown into an overcrowded women's prison where the stench made her gag and where there wasn't enough room to lie down without touching another's body. The tears she cried that night weren't for herself, however. They were for Ramona and Beatriz. Ramona would grow up not remembering her mother. And Beatriz would never know what had become of her daughter. Carmelita carried a new burden, she had failed them both.

CHAPTER 26

That day Beatriz stayed in bed. Her entire being convulsed by thoughts of her little girl, alone and wanting her mother, transported far away to another part of the country where Beatriz couldn't find her.

Beatriz's heart was a rock inside her, so heavy that she didn't know how she could go on weighed down with such grief. She ignored her mother's entreaties to eat something. Finally, come evening she roused herself and nibbled half-heartedly on some bread and olives.

The house had become a morgue, silent and lifeless without Ramona running around, shouting, laughing. The child had been Beatriz's angel. Ramona brought joy where there'd been none. She was the future but now the boots of fascism had ground Beatriz's future into the dust.

When night fell, she thought about Carmelita. "Did she not come home this afternoon?"

"No," answered her mother in a tone which indicated she considered it would be a good thing if Carmelita never returned.

The next morning, concerned for Carmelita's safety, Beatriz threw on some clothes and walked across town to the street where Carmelita had told her she worked. Passing a young girl holding her mother's hand, Beatriz's lips trembled and her eyes misted.

She knocked on the house with the large doors Carmelita had described. One opened only slightly until half of a woman's face was visible. "Yes?"

"I was wondering if this is where my friend, Carmelita, works. She didn't come home last night and I'm worried about her."

"She doesn't work here any longer, I dismissed her over a week ago." The door shut.

Beatriz wondered why Carmelita hadn't mentioned that she'd lost her job and what else she was doing when she went out while still pretending to go to work. Beatriz knew going to the police would be a waste of time. Under Franco's regime, people disappeared every day, arrested on the slightest pretext and often never to be heard from again.

A sudden thought about her daughter seized her being. On a rush of hope, Beatriz hurried to the Town Hall and waited outside. He must appear soon, leaving for siesta. If anyone could help her, it was him. When he came out of the building she accosted him.

"I want my daughter," she demanded.

"I don't know what you're on about," said Francisco.

"The Falangists took her. You have connections, you can get her back for me. If you do, I'll be your mistress." The prospect revolted Beatriz but it was a price worth paying.

"I've already told you, I know nothing. And you flatter yourself if you think I still desire you. Now get out of my way." He forcefully pushed her to one side.

"I'll find out where you live and tell your wife about how you behaved!"

The man stopped in his tracks, and came back to her until his face was almost touching hers, his eyes on fire. "If you come anywhere near our home or if you ever bother me or my wife, you'll never dance again. All it takes is an accusation from me that you're a leftist and a judge will lock you up for decades."

Powerless and defeated, Beatriz watched him go. She headed back towards Triana. How she resented the bright, cheerful sunshine and the pretty lilac blooms hanging from the jacaranda trees. She wanted to hide away in a shroud of dark shadow. Living had lost its purpose.

Many times Beatriz considered ending it all but she didn't. While the pain was always present, she eventually found a way to cope. She returned once more to her first love. Flamenco provided an escape, a way to forget. When she danced, the concentration required drove thoughts of loss from her mind.

Beatriz practised all morning and danced all

evening. It was exhausting but exhaustion reduced the number of sleepless nights. And maybe one day, she would tell herself, she would be able to fight back against those who now ruled this country and inflicted so much misery. Beatriz didn't care if she died in the process. So long as she did something to avenge her suffering, and the suffering of the countless thousands of the other victims, it would make her death worthwhile.

In Paris, Ramon waited impatiently for the European-wide war which Luis had predicted. Ramon fantasised about Franco being overthrown and returning to his family and Beatriz. It was a hope that got him out of bed each morning. After a day's work, he would join his colleagues in a bar near the office to discuss how they would transform Spain when they returned, their conversations becoming louder and more boisterous while the evening progressed and the number of empty wine bottles grew.

One Monday morning in early September 1939, Ramon arrived at the office to find everyone hugging and smiling. "It's happening!" Luis shouted out to him across the room. "The war we wanted has begun."

It was as if a damp and bone-chilling three year long fog had lifted. A sun of freedom was about to breach the horizon.

"Yes!" Arms aloft, Ramon jumped in the air for joy.

"Now we have only to wait," Luis told him. "Hitler

will call in the debt Franco owes him for the men and weapons he provided, particularly his ruthless bombing of our country by his Condor Legion. And Franco wants Gibraltar back. If he succeeds the fascists, not the British, will control the entrance to the Mediterranean. We will be contacting the French and British governments to offer our whole-hearted support. And if they agree to provide us with arms, we can prepare an invasion force at the border to be ready to move at a moment's notice."

"I want to be part of that."

"You will be, as soon as the time comes."

Yet months passed and Spain remained neutral.

"That bastard Franco is a wily old fox, he's waiting to see which way the wind is blowing. But Germany is advancing so that will likely tip the balance and make him declare war on the Allies," Luis assured Ramon in April 1940. Franco would, however, keep Spain officially neutral during the Second World War.

Paris transformed herself into a city on a war footing. Sandbags protected major buildings and soldiers guarded them. While he cycled to work in early June, Ramon could hear what sounded like distant thunder but was too regular and repetitive to be that. The traffic was unusually light and the streets almost deserted.

When he reached the office, he encountered a state of pandemonium. The air was hot from a roaring fireplace into which staff were throwing papers. Many of the former government ministers were nowhere to be seen. Luis remained but his cheeriness of recent months was gone and beads of perspiration coated his forehead.

"The Germans are on the outskirts of the city, and they say France is about to surrender and let them into Paris to avoid the city's destruction. Many of my colleagues have gone home to pack and head for the coast to find a boat out. Mexico has offered to take us all. There's nothing for you to do today, come back in the morning and you can leave with the rest of us."

That evening, Ramon ventured out and wandered the streets of Montmartre. Normally there would be couples embracing in shop doorways, lively music and loud applause coming from the Moulin Rouge and other venues, crowds spilling out onto the streets from the packed bars. Tonight there was an absence of people, an unnatural quiet and an eerie emptiness. Life had been sucked out of the city.

It was past midnight when Ramon returned to his room. He'd made up his mind. He didn't want to go to Mexico. It had the feeling of a permanent exile, a confirmation that he was never going to see his homeland again. Ramon would stay and find a way to join the French resistance which would surely be formed when the country fell.

It was already late when Ramon woke. He mounted his bicycle and cycled down the hill. He wanted to tell Luis of his decision to stay and wish the man good luck.

It wasn't long before he saw them. Nazi troopers marching along the main boulevards, the noise of their jackboots ricocheting off walls and creating an ominous atmosphere of impending doom. Ramon kept to the back streets to reach the office. He tore up the stairs two by two and flung open the door.

"Ah, another traitor arrives," announced a man dressed in a black uniform, knee high boots, and a black cap bearing a skull and crossbones. Members of the Gestapo were boxing up papers while Luis and those who failed to leave yesterday stood in silence against the wall, their faces frozen with fear. "I expect you might be wondering why an officer of the Reich speaks Spanish. My team has been tasked with rounding up the enemies of El Caudillo in Paris to deliver them safe and sound to the care of the legitimate Spanish government. Join the others. Now!" The man barked, annoyed at Ramon's lack of immediate compliance with his command.

CHAPTER 27

On their return to Spain, Luis and others with past involvement in government were sentenced to death after only the briefest of trials where the judges allowed no time for the defendants to speak. Ramon was sentenced to thirty years in prison and wished he, too, had been shot. He tried not to think about the future. He no longer had one. He would be old by the time he was released, his life wasted and pointless.

In addition to the many thousands who were executed, over three hundred thousand would be imprisoned. Conditions were appalling and many would die from hunger and disease.

On a bitter winter's morning, penetrating rain soaked Ramon. Like fingers of ice, cold drops found their way down the back of his neck. He shivered while he stood in the prison compound with the hundreds of other inmates in their threadbare clothing. They were forced to sing, raise their voices in praise of the man who had decreed they should live in misery. Sing the compulsory Francoist anthems which mocked their wretchedness.

The camp commander announced he brought good news for them. Ramon expected it was likely to be sadistic sarcasm. The man only ever demanded that they work harder and had already cut their meagre rations twice.

"El Caudillo has revealed plans for a memorial to our blessed martyrs who saved Spain from Communism. In his own words, 'it will be the greatest temple of the dead for our heroes to rest'. And in his benevolence, he is offering you the chance of redemption. Each day worked on building this marvel for future generations to admire, and where they will come to pay their respects, will result in six days off your sentence. Those of you who wish to participate, line up against the wall."

Every able bodied man quickly did so. Ramon experienced a surge of hope for the first time since Paris. If he worked on this project for five years, he would have completed his sentence and be released. Five years was a long time but a whole lot less than thirty. He would still be young with most of his life in front of him and, with luck, Beatriz would still be waiting for him.

That same day, he and the others were marched from the prison on the outskirts of Madrid for fifty kilometres across the bleak and windswept high plateau of the Meseta Central to the Sierra de Guadarrama where a large prison camp had been hastily and poorly erected. The scantest regard paid to the protection of its inmates from the inhospitable climate where winters were brutal and summers Sahara-like in their intensity.

The following morning, the men were taken to a rock face of inscrutable grey. It towered above them, impregnable and immoveable. Told that it was here they were to burrow and create an interior to house a Basilica which would be a quarter of a kilometre in length, longer even than St Peter's in the Vatican, Ramon's spirits plummeted.

It came without sufficient warning like it always did. There was only the briefest of rumbles or the creaking of a wooden support before huge lumps of rock rained down as if the world was ending. Ramon turned and ran.

When quiet returned, he and the others who had got away entered a huge cloud of dust, coughing like asthmatics while they removed fallen rubble with bare and bleeding hands. Mostly they pulled out corpses. The bodies of the few who remained alive were so mutilated that death would have been a blessing.

Day after endless day, Ramon and thousands of others continued to toil on this work of pharaonic construction like the slaves who built the pyramids, creating a memorial to their oppressors intended to last as long as the monuments of ancient Egypt. Ramon soon realised he had again made a pact with the devil but he didn't regret it.

Should he die in an accident, it was better than his previous prospect of thirty years incarceration.

In Seville, Beatriz continued dancing and receiving acclaim. She would gladly have traded her success for getting her daughter back, but she knew she must accept that wasn't going to happen. Although she smiled for her audience, in her heart there would always be the shadow of sorrow no matter how radiantly the Sevillian sun shone day after day.

When her mother announced she was leaving to live with her sister in Granada, Beatriz didn't try to persuade her to stay. Beatriz didn't worry about being alone, she already felt lonely with her mother as company. Their relationship, never easy at the best of times, had become worse without Carmelita and Ramona to provide relief from her mother's endless criticism.

"I think it's a good idea," said Beatriz. "Here, you're on your own all day, what with me practising each morning, out every evening, and sleeping during the afternoon."

"You just want to be rid of me," accused her mother. Beatriz didn't respond.

It was several years after the Civil War when a man in military uniform approached the stage at the end of a performance.

"Señorita, may I have a moment of your time?"

Beatriz glared at him. "Do I have a choice?"

"Indeed you do but what I have to ask would

increase your fame and earning potential greatly."

Beatriz was intrigued. "Meet me outside in five minutes."

The man was leaning against a wall and smoking a cigar when she appeared. Beatriz was forthright, she'd had to learn how to stand up for herself in a society where women weren't expected to question their fate. "What is it then? I don't have time to waste."

"In that case, I'll get straight to the point. His Excellency, El Caudillo, is visiting Seville next month and has expressed a wish to watch flamenco. You are recognised as one of the most accomplished dancers in our city and your name has therefore been suggested."

This was news Beatriz hadn't expected but she didn't refuse. "All right, I'll do it."

"Good, I should have the details confirmed in a couple of days. How do I contact you?"

"Come back here. If I'm not around, speak to Manuel in the ticket office. He'll be able to pass on your message."

Izil watched the parched summer landscape of Spain pass by from the window of the train, a landscape the sun had roasted and which bore the hues of Africa not Europe. La Guardia Mora were accompanying Franco, who was up front in a much more luxurious carriage. They were going to Cordoba and then on to Seville. Izil had wanted to visit Cordoba ever since Brahim had regaled him with tales of its magnificence under Moorish rule, the greatest city in Spain and the whole of Europe in the days of Al-Andalus.

In recognition of the contribution made by his Muslim Africanistas, Franco had consented to the building of a mosque in Cordoba, Al-Morabito, the first to be constructed in Spain for over five hundred years. The men were given permission to go there to worship. Izil imagined a large dome and minarets reaching towards the heavens.

Walking from the station, the excitement Izil and his colleagues experienced grew as they scoured the skyline for their first glimpse. When they arrived at the mosque, they were sorely disappointed. There wasn't even a single minaret, and the whitewashed building with a blue dome was small and unimpressive.

"Is this all they give us after what we've done for them?" complained one of Izil's colleagues. "Thousands of our brothers die and we get a mosque no bigger than can be found in any Moroccan village. It's an insult."

After the sermon from the Imam, the men strolled around the city. Izil became detached from the group and explored alone. Ahead, he saw what looked like La Giralda in Seville and wondered if it, too, would once have been a minaret.

Izil walked through an archway built in the classic Islamic style. It went straight up for a few metres and was crowned with a horseshoe arch. He entered a large rectangular courtyard of orange trees, similar to Seville Cathedral's 'el Patio de los Naranjos' which dated from when there had been a mosque.

In front of Izil lounged a huge but unremarkable building of desert coloured stone, flat roofed from this angle with a church-type structure supplanted upon part of it. It was as if an alien spaceship had landed there, so incongruous was the addition to the original building. Izil knew instinctively he must be looking at what once was the fabled Great Mosque of Cordoba built over a thousand years ago.

Inside, a he found a forest of double horseshoe arches on supporting pillars of granite jasper and marble. They were mesmerising in their profusion and brought a sense of infinity to the interior. There are said to be eight hundred and fifty of them. Sunlight streamed in, and in their alternate brick and stone pattern which created a red and white stripe effect, the arches were breathtaking. Izil's heart beat faster, enthralled to think his ancestors had created this marvel.

Towards the centre, a nave had been thrust, a gothic-style vault with the usual carvings of apostles and angels, intruding on this wonder of the world. The visible dominance of Christianity over Islam dampened Izil's mood and he wandered back into the maze of Islamic archways which became polylobed.

To his side, he noticed a mihrab, the wall in a mosque which faces in the direction of prayer.

To get the best possible view, he pressed himself against the gate of metal railings which closed off access. Beyond was a magnificent archway surrounded by cobalt blue and gold with Kufic lettering, an older and upright form of Arabic script, containing passages from the Koran.

Looking upwards, he saw a dazzling dome of gold mosaic as if a flower of paradise. Overcome with emotion, Izil drew back and fell to his knees and bent his head forward to touch the ground in prayer.

Angry shouts interrupted his meditation. Two men grabbed him roughly by the arms and dragged him prostrate across the stone floor, ignoring his protests.

"How dare you defile the house of God!" cried one. Reaching a side door, they flung him out into the street.

Izil got up and dusted himself down, boiling with resentment. He couldn't live this way any longer, dressed up like a performing monkey to satisfy Franco's delusions of grandeur. The current period of service Izil had signed up for would end shortly and he decided then and there he wouldn't renew it. It was time to return to Morocco.

CHAPTER 28

Slowly the monument to Franco's dead soldiers was beginning to take shape, but it was apparent it would take years to complete, another decade or longer. Ramon had been counting the days since his arrival, backbreaking days of hard labour, five long years. It was time for his release. That was the only thing which kept Ramon going through what had been the darkest days of his life.

For each day worked, he was paid the miserly sum of three pesetas. One peseta was taken for his food, one supposedly to send to his family, and one put aside for him. He consoled himself thinking there should now be over fifteen hundred pesetas in his name, enough to get back to Andalusia and survive while he looked for work. He would finally be free, or as free as anyone could be under Franco's regime.

Finishing his shift, Ramon dragged his blistered feet towards the prison camp. His hair was caked with grit, his limbs bruised, and his hands covered in cuts and scabs. He'd waited long enough, it was time to ask. Diffidently, Ramon knocked on the door of the camp commander's office and entered.

"What do you want?" The voice was gruff and the man glowered at him from behind his desk.

"We were told that each day worked here would count as a reduction of six days from our sentence. I've been here for over five years and have therefore served my time."

"What you were told was wrong, it's a reduction of one day for every three days worked. Now get out before I have you thrown into solitary."

Ramon staggered across the yard, feeling as if he'd been punched in the stomach and kicked in the head. Their promises were lies, damn lies. He faced another fifteen years, perhaps his whole sentence. If they could lie once, they could lie again.

Beatriz was lost to him now. How could her love endure over twenty years of separation? Ramon knew she wanted a family, something she would be too old for if she waited for him. She'd probably met someone already, and if not soon would.

Back in the hut he shared with so many others, Ramon collapsed onto his bed of straw. He felt the fleas bite but Ramon wanted never to get up again. But he did, they all did. There was no choice in the matter.

Beatriz applied the finishing touches to her makeup and looked at herself in the mirror. A fierce pride in her heritage reflected back at her. It was an image of Spain Franco wanted to present to the world. That flamenco was strongest amongst

Spain's despised gitano community was an irony lost on him.

The dress she had taken from her cupboard for the occasion was black with red polka dots and white lace trimming on each of the frills on the lower half and ended just above her ankles. Beatriz had chosen a dress she could easily run in. When she lunged at the man she would be able to do it with such speed that no one would have time to stop her. Once more she practised slipping her hand under the uppermost frill and pulling her father's dagger swiftly from the padded pocket she had sown beneath.

Her hand was steady. She'd expected to be nervous but she wasn't. This was her destiny, to rid the world of the evil dictator. It would be for Ramona and Carmelita wherever they might be, and for her brother, and the hundreds of thousands murdered in cold blood.

She walked across Puente de Isabel and looked down for a final time on the Guadalquivir. The river was sparkling and carefree in the brilliant sunshine, untroubled by the unending conflicts of mankind. Turning right, she crossed the traffic such as it was. Donkeys with baskets slung either side of their backs and horses and carts still outnumbered motor vehicles. The war may have ended several years ago but Spain remained poorer than before it began.

Outside the massive oval Plaza de Toros, the bull ring, painted in yellow, red, and white, Beatriz hired one of the city's black four-wheeled open carriages pulled by a handsome chestnut brown horse. She would make her last journey in style.

As the carriage took the street between the Cathedral and the Archivo de Indias and into Plaza del Triunfo, her heart rate increased until it was beating faster than the clip-clop of the horses' hooves. Beatriz was nearly there and her earlier sang-froid was giving way to panic. Save for when her father had attacked her, she'd never used a dagger. Be calm, she told herself. You can do this. You must do this. Approach him slowly while you dance. Draw his eyes to yours. Let him see the hatred, then charge at him. Stab him in the heart, stab him repeatedly, again and again until they drag you off him or shoot you.

The carriage pulled up at La Puerta del Leon, the Lion's Gate, at the Alcazar Real, Seville's royal palace, and the oldest one in Europe. Above the gate, ceramic tiles depicted a lion wearing a crown and holding a cross in his right paw. Beatriz had never been inside this place and its extensive grounds secluded from view by high walls.

When Beatriz entered the first courtyard, a man stepped out from the shadows dressed in a turban and cloak. It was as if she'd been transported back a thousand years.

"You must be the dancer?" Beatriz nodded. "El Caudillo is running late, may I show you around to pass the time?"

"Yes, that would be interesting." Beatriz thought

she sounded shrill and hoped he hadn't detected the nervousness in her voice.

"First, I must check you. It's standard security."

Beatriz tensed as he ran his hands down the side of her tight-fitting top half and proceeded down her dress. When he finished, she exhaled.

Izil's suspicion was aroused. "I need to do it again." This time Izil stopped against a frill. His hand touched something solid. He lifted the frill and pulled out the dagger. The blade glinted accusingly in the sunlight.

Beatriz's cheeks became hot and she knew she must be blushing. "I forgot to take it out. I carry it in case customers get carried away or try following me home after a late night performance. It's happened a couple of times, but they backed off when I showed them the knife."

"I'll need to take it. You can have it back when you leave."

Beatriz's initial relief at his reaction was swept aside by frustration and disappointment. That brute Franco would live and continue inflicting his misery. She had failed, failed all those who had died because of him and all those who continued to suffer.

"Come. My name is Izil, I am a member of His Excellency's Guardia Mora."

He led her through ground floor rooms with exquisite tiles and arches of such delicate stonework it was as though they were made from lace. Beatriz thought this was what the

Islamic world must look like. Although rebuilt by Christian monarchs after they'd driven the Moors from Seville, Arab architects had been employed to create the world's leading example of 'Mudejar', a fusion of Islamic and Christian influences.

In the gardens, a fountain shot several metres into the air falling back into a large pool and giving an illusion of coolness. They wandered pathways beneath soaring palms, and cypresses, amongst orange and lemon trees, and past exotic cerise-pink hibiscus in an awkward silence which Izil was the first to break.

"I'm not stupid, I know what you intended to do." Beatriz avoided the piercing gaze of his coffee coloured eyes. "But there's no need to worry, I'm not going to tell. I also loathe Franco and his regime."

Beatriz let her tightened shoulders drop. "Then why do you work for him?"

"I was one of thousands of poor young Moroccans who signed up so their families wouldn't starve. And from what we were led to believe, we thought that at last we'd be treated as equals and no longer be looked down upon. But nothing's changed, we're still the underdogs."

"So are gitanos. I just happen to escape a lot of the prejudice because I became a popular dancer. And you, aren't you a special case in all your finery as part of his elite guard?"

"I'm paid better that's for sure, and while we're with him no one insults us. But out of these clothes, I get the verbal and physical attacks all Moroccans are on the receiving end of. We should probably get back now, I expect Franco will be arriving soon."

Izil led Beatriz through a wide archway from outside into the Salon de Embajadores, the Hall of Ambassadors. The guitar player and the man who sang at the venue where she often performed were already there. In this room, Kings and Queens of Spain had received important visitors, and today a high-backed chair in red velvet stood upon a dais ready for the arrival of Spain's new absolute monarch in all but name, officials lined up on either side.

While waiting Beatriz had time to appreciate the room, grander still than the impressive ones Izil had shown her earlier. Square in shape, it had three Islamic style horseshoe arches on the three other walls which led to other parts of the Alcazar. Tiles from Triana adorned the walls at low level giving way to a more Islamic feel of intricate stone patterns higher up. Immediately below the ceiling was a gilded frieze with paintings of Spain's monarchs. The stunning climax of the room was its ceiling. A golden star shape was largely obscured by a circular dome of gilded wood, symbolising the heavens and inlaid with precious stones. Beatriz couldn't help but be awestruck.

Moments later the sound of marching becoming ever nearer ended the tranquility. Members of La Guardia Mora swept in followed by Franco in knee-high boots and his olive green military uniform with a sash of red and yellow diagonally positioned across his upper body. He ascended onto the dais to appear taller than he was and sat down. Looking at Beatriz with only the hint of a smile he pushed out his right arm, palm upward, to indicate she should begin.

Normally Beatriz was able to give a dramatic and authentic performance by dancing herself into a trance like state as if she were no longer an earthly being, but today she struggled to get there, to find 'duende'. While she moved she thought of how this should have been the moment when she secured revenge for his victims, ending the dictator's life and changing history. She fixed her eyes on Franco like a witch casting a spell. The intensity of her glare made him shift uncomfortably in his seat.

At the end Franco clapped politely as did his entourage, but the applause was muted and he left without thanking Beatriz. Not that she minded, making small talk with him would have been anathema to her. A man whose military coup had resulted in half a million deaths and incalculable misery. Although she had been unable to kill him, Beatriz took some comfort from the thought he was probably a superstitious man who might now be worried she had placed a curse on him.

Izil escorted her back to La Puerta del Leon. Retrieving her dagger from a side room, he presented it to her with outstretched hands and a bow of his head.

"I hope you will never need to use it." Beatriz couldn't help but grin. "Would you care to meet for a drink this evening?"

"Why not," responded Beatriz. "Meet me at the Seville end of the iron bridge at eight."

CHAPTER 29

Izil had changed out of his ceremonial garb into beige trousers and a white shirt. Beatriz looked much less dramatic than she had at the Alcazar, arriving in a pale pink dress with short sleeves. She suggested they go to a bar, but when Izil explained he didn't drink alcohol, she took him to an open air cafe in Parque de Maria Luisa where they drank freshly squeezed orange juice while swallows swooped and caught insects on the wing.

"Aren't you just a little bit sorry you found the knife?" asked Beatriz.

"Absolutely not or we wouldn't be having this drink together. You'd be dead or suffering indescribable torture. Tell me, why were you seeking vengeance, did they kill a member of your family?"

"Yes, more than one, and they also took away the person I loved most."

"I'm sorry."

"And you, how long will you continue working for these devils?"

"My current contract ends soon and I don't intend

to renew it. I plan to return to Morocco."

"I've always wanted to go there. I've heard it's beautiful."

"It is, you'd like it. And I hope one day soon my country will be free."

Beatriz suggested they walk around the park. She was attracted to Izil. There was an authenticity to him she found appealing.

"We're staying in Seville until the day after tomorrow. I was hoping you might be free to meet up again," said Izil.

"I'm working tomorrow night. Why don't you come and watch, and we could get something to eat afterwards."

The following night they ended up strolling through the park once again after their meal. Even though it was past midnight, the air stroked their skin with a sensual warmth. When it came time to say goodbye, Izil placed a tentative kiss upon her lips. It awakened an inner desire which Beatriz hadn't felt for such a long while. She responded with passion, pulling him close. Holding him reminded her how much she missed the human touch and the comfort it brought.

"Can I come and see you again on my way to Morocco in a month's time?" asked Izil.

"Of course."

"Where do you live?"

Beatriz imagined how the neighbours would gossip if he were to visit her house.

"Come to the same club as tonight. I'm dancing

there every day of the week except Sundays for the next couple of months."

In the filth and degradation of prison, Carmelita turned to God to survive. Once a week, nuns were allowed to visit. Their starched white cornettes with wing-like protrusions at the sides made them appear like a female version of the Civil Guards and their winged hats. Many of the women refused to have anything to do with them.

"They're the evil hand maidens of the Catholic Church which sided with Franco and failed to protect the poor and vulnerable," one of the inmates spat out in disgust. "I prefer to remain in this shit hole rather than spend time with them."

Carmelita, however, accepted their invitation to prayer. Not only was she allowed out into the prison yard where the air didn't stink so badly but she found hope in their message salvation was possible. Carmelita needed that. If she accepted this wretched life was all she had, and after death there was nothing, Carmelita knew she wouldn't be able to cope any longer. Already her emotions teetered daily on a cliff of despair. Her life had always been difficult but not to this degree. Here there was no opportunity to take a walk to shake off the demons hitching a ride on her back, no chance to see beauty of any sort and feel better for it.

One particular sister took an interest in Carmelita. She asked Carmelita why she was imprisoned.

Still fearing what the consequences might be for Beatriz, she lied.

"I love children and have always wanted to be a mother. However, I never will be so I tried to steal my employer's child. I know it was wrong but I couldn't help myself."

The sister placed her hand on Carmelita's. "Yes, it was wrong but God forgives sinners who truly repent. God has made you who you are for a reason and you must accept that. There are ways to serve him other than through motherhood. Have you ever thought of devoting your life to him when you get out of here?"

Carmelita was astonished at the suggestion. "Surely the church doesn't want someone like me, deformed and a convict?"

"As I said, God forgives those who repent. How much longer until you're freed?"

"Another four years."

"Then we have plenty of time to prepare you. I could teach you to read. I take it you can't."

"No."

"We shall begin next week." The woman was so certain of herself that Carmelita didn't think to question her plan.

Carmelita enjoyed learning to read from the Bible. The stories transported her over the high prison walls to strange and exotic lands where God performed miracles, and where those who were good were saved and those who were evil incurred his wrath. It was a world which appealed to her, a world where she could belong and no longer be an outcast.

Standing behind her daughter while she stood in front of the full length mirror in her bedroom, tears welled in Luisa's eyes.
"You look so beautiful, Carmen. I can't believe how you're growing up so fast."
Carmen's white dress came almost to her ankles and the long sleeves were made of lace. Her mother arranged Carmen's thick black hair in a bun on top of her head and attached the top of her headdress to it.
Carmen beamed at her reflection. Carmen didn't know she'd been born Ramona. She retained no recollection of her abduction from her home in Triana, of kicking and screaming, of trying to bite the man who'd picked her up and held her in the vice of his arms. Nor did she retain any memory of her real mother.
Today would be such a special day, her first Holy Communion, to be taken in the Cathedral and administered by His Eminence, Cardinal Segura.
Francisco was a proud man as, head held high, he led his wife and daughter towards the ringing bells and the huge doors above which stone carvings of saints gazed down upon them. All was right with the world. Spain had been saved from the godless dystopia of Communism, and he and his wife had found their heart's desire in Carmen, a child to love and dote upon.

On his landed estate, the workers no longer dared to agitate for higher pay and shorter hours. Order had been restored and things were like they were meant to be. The troublemakers were either dead or in prison.

Carmen was also enjoying the occasion but she preferred their normal weekend routine when they would drive out to the family's hacienda in the country. There she got to ride a horse, her very own jet black mare which her parents had given her earlier in the year. That too had been a truly memorable day.

Each day after Christmas, she was allowed to move the three kings, who formed part of the family's hand-carved nativity set displayed on the oak sideboard in the living room, a little closer to the other characters. By Epiphany on the fifth day of January they were at the stable with Joseph, Mary, and baby Jesus.

That evening with her mother and father she joined the crowds on the streets of Seville to watch the annual Parade of the Three Kings, la Cabalgata de los Reyes Magos. Her eyes, like those of the other children, shone with wonder to see the three men on camels, with crowns on their turbans and cloaks of shimmering gold, red, and green. Those preceding them threw sweets at the children. They all knew that tomorrow was the day when finally the long wait would be over, the day in Spain when Christmas presents were given. This wasn't the land of Father Christmas, but a country where centuries old religious traditions of the festive season remained firmly sown into the fabric of life.

Normally the family stayed in Seville, but this year her parents had driven her to their country home after the parade while she slept, dreaming of the evening's spectacle.

The following morning, her face fell when she ran into her parent's bedroom in her nightdress expecting to see wrapped gifts only to find there were none.

"Don't worry, cariño," said Francisco, ruffling her hair affectionately. "Your present is in a different place this year. Get dressed and we shall join you in the entrance hall in a few minutes."

Hand in hand with their daughter, they led her towards the stables. She clasped their hands tightly with unadulterated joy, having already guessed why they were taking her there.

"You're the best parents in the whole world, I'm so lucky to have you as my mother and father," she exclaimed when they introduced her to her horse. Carmen stroked the mare's face and lay hers against it. Her life was perfect.

CHAPTER 30

Beatriz found herself thinking less about Ramona and of Izil instead. He was undeniably handsome and somewhat mysterious. His face spoke of a world that wasn't European, of those mysterious lands her ancestors travelled across long ago to reach Spain.

Yet it also filled her with guilt to be considering the possibility of love when she didn't know who was taking care of her daughter and whether she was safe and happy. Many a time Beatriz wanted to scream with frustration that she would never have an answer to that question. At other times, she dissolved into sobs of despair. Her complete powerlessness to do anything to change the situation still gnawed at her day and night.

Izil returned, taking a room in a small hotel in Santa Cruz overlooking the ancient walls of the Alcazar constructed during the time of Muslim rule. Behind the walls tall palm trees reached for the sky, a sky which was obscured by an orange haze. A southerly wind had carried billions of dust and sand particles from the Sahara. Izil considered it to be a good omen.

In the sultry heat which lingered on into late September, their love ignited. Lying in his arms during siesta, Beatriz found a peace she hadn't experienced since Ramona had been snatched from her. Come evening, they would wander hand in hand to a local restaurant where Beatriz would nibble on a few morsels from his plate.

"Dancing and a full stomach don't mix," she told him. Beatriz would then leave at ten to do a show and return to their love nest after midnight.

Their secret world was cosy and secure but they both understood it could only be temporary. Reality couldn't be kept at bay for long.

"I must leave tomorrow. Come with me," urged Izil while he sat with his back against the red velvet headboard. "You'd like Tetouan, it's a charming mixture of Spain and Morocco. I could make you happy there."

"But what would I do?"

"Become my wife."

Beatriz sat up in bed. "I can't."

"Why not? What's here for you, other than a mother you say you've nothing in common with and who lives in Granada? Don't you want to settle down and have a family?"

Beatriz inhaled and pursed her lips together before speaking to contain her emotions. "I already have a daughter."

"Why did you never mention her?"

"Because it's too painful. She was stolen from me

when she was only two years old by the Fascists, and taken to an orphanage to be placed with a Francoist family somewhere else in Spain. She'll be eight by now. There's not a day, not a waking hour, that I don't think about her."

"That must be hard to bear. And the father, I take it you're not together or is there another secret you haven't told me?" There was a note of jealous resentment in Izil's voice.

"He doesn't know she exists. He left Seville when the civil war began and never returned."

Izil picked up her hand and kissed it. "Difficult as it must be to accept, you're never going to get her back."

"Perhaps, yet there's always a chance that one day I'll get some news and be able to see her. That's why I must stay here, in case."

"But-"

"You can't change my mind." Her eyes were opaque and uncompromising.

At dinner that evening their conversation didn't flow easily like it always had. It was punctuated by long silences but not of the natural kind lovers share. When Beatriz returned to the room after her show, Izil had already departed.

Izil stood at the bow for the whole journey, breathing in the seductive scent of Africa carried on the breeze and enjoying the sea spray on his face. He focussed resolutely on the rugged mountains beyond the coastline. Not once did he glance back. His heart would mend more quickly the sooner he forgot about her.

Spain was Al-Shaytan, the devil, tempting with a dangerous passion and casting aside those who succumbed to it. Izil's future would be bright if he was strong and ignored the incessant whisperings of Al-Shaytan in his ear. He had left his homeland impoverished and was coming back a wealthy man by local standards.

From the port, Izil took a bus to Tetouan, packed not only with noisy passengers but also clucking hens and a bleating goat. Teenage boys sat on the roof, their legs dangling over the windows. The chaos made Izil smile and confirmed he was home. He began a search for a place to live amongst the white sugar cube like buildings of the old town. The moment he entered the peaceful inner courtyard of blue and white tiles with a fountain and a fig tree he knew he'd found his home.

Izil rented premises in the nearby medina and opened a cafe. Men came to gossip while they drank mint tea and smoked hookah pipes. It was a place for them to escape the pungent, penetrating smell of urine, rotting flesh, and stagnant water coming from the nearby open air tannery. Many of Izil's customers were former Africanistas, and together they shared stories of their time in Spain. It wasn't long until his friend, Brahim, visited. "I heard you were back. So you finally came to join the struggle."

"From what I've picked up, it seems to be all talk."

"It takes time, I'm busy establishing contacts with like minded souls in French Morocco."

"Well, let me know when you have something concrete to propose. For now, I need to concentrate on my business and finding a wife."

When Izil had persuaded his mother to join him, she'd spoken of little else.

"Even your younger brother and sister have already wed. Tafrara's expecting her first baby. It's time you got a move on. I shall make enquiries." This time Izil didn't argue with her.

Izil's bride was suitably demure and willing to let his mother rule the roost. There were occasions when Izil thought of Beatriz. He missed her fiery and independent nature, but he knew living between two worlds was unlikely to bring lasting happiness.

Izil spent most of his waking hours in his cafe, except when at the mosque. The call to prayers by the muezzin was reassuring, something he realised he had sorely missed across the water where only the bells of the Catholic Church were permitted.

CHAPTER 31

For months, whenever a southerly wind blew hot air in from the South, Beatriz thought of Morocco. A land she had never seen but which existed vividly in her imagination. A place of narrow alleyways, offering the occasional glimpse of private courtyards where women in brightly coloured clothing sat free of their drab djellabas and face coverings. In the air, the exotic aroma of spices, and a caravan of camels languidly leaving town, their riders responding to the call of the desert and welcoming the prospect of sleeping under stars too numerous to count.

Beatriz's feelings for Izil still flickered along with a nagging doubt that she should have gone with him, that a life in a country so different would have healed the hole in her heart Ramona's absence had created. As time passed, she knew she'd made the right decision. Her pain would have been greater in a place her daughter would never come looking, even though the chances of Ramona ever knowing where she came from were slim.

Beatriz accepted the cold embrace of a life without

love. She enjoyed her independence and rejected all advances. She'd decided that to entangle herself in a marriage she might well come to regret would be foolish.

In Franco's Spain, women had no rights. Divorce was unlawful and so was birth control. Women no longer had the vote and were required to obey their husbands in all matters. They were expected to be mothers and homemakers. Anyone could accuse them of immoral behaviour, which could result in being sent to a reformatory. Beatriz was determined to steer clear of such traps. She counted herself lucky her dancing enabled her to have a career.

Not knowing for how much longer she would remain in demand as a performer, Beatriz opened a flamenco school. Those who lived in Triana had no spare money to spend on lessons so she found a room to rent near the fine arts museum in Seville and passed out cards to attract the daughters of wealthier residents. It was several months until she began to make a profit, but word spread and the number of her students grew.

There were days when Beatriz found teaching difficult and had to call upon all her inner strength to get through a lesson. She couldn't help but think of Ramona when she looked at the girls who came to be taught. Those eager, smiling faces, girls who at the end of class ran into the arms of their mothers waiting by the door. How Beatriz wished she still had Ramona to rush into her empty arms.

Beatriz could only hope and pray her daughter was happy and that the family she lived with was kind and loving.

It was a Saturday morning. Mother and daughter were out shopping for new clothes, not that they'd found anything Luisa liked.

"There'll be a much better choice when we go to Paris next month," she told Carmen. The Castillo family continued to enjoy a life of privilege few Spaniards got to experience.

They paused outside a building to listen to the furious foot stomping coming from within.

"Flamenco," commented Luisa.

"Can I learn?" asked Carmen.

"Maybe when you're older."

Carmen persisted. "But I'm already twelve. Look, there's some cards over there." Carmen went across to the small table by the open door. Picking up a card, she peeped inside. The teacher was demonstrating to her students.

Carmen was immediately captivated by the woman. She was so poised, so striking. When she moved it was with such grace and assurance, her head held high, her back ramrod straight and her arms extended. Carmen's impulsive desire to learn became something much more intense. She wanted to be like that woman.

"Beatriz is the teacher's name." Carmen handed the card to her mother. "Please say yes." She put her hands together as if in prayer.

"You can go if your father approves."

Carmen smiled, she knew exactly how to wrap him around her little finger. At dinner that evening she waited until he had finished his dessert. With a full stomach, his mood was at its best.

"Papa, I saw something today I really want to do." She gave him that sweet, innocent look which always won him over, using her eyes and tilting her head like a puppy.

"And what might that be?"

"I want to learn flamenco."

"A woman named Beatriz runs the class," interjected her mother.

Francisco's expression changed from one of mild interest to one of fury.

"Absolutely not! I forbid it. Flamenco is for gitanas and loose women."

"That isn't so. El Caudillo approves of it, he says it's an important part of Spanish culture," protested Carmen.

"For peasants, maybe. I will not have a daughter of mine becoming a dancer."

"But-"

"Go to your room! I've heard quite enough from you for one evening, and don't ever mention it again."

Carmen burst into tears and ran out, hurt and confused by her father's reaction.

"Was that really necessary?" Luisa chided him.

"I blame you for putting such a notion in her head." Scowling, he pushed his chair back. "I need to get back to the office, I have work I must finish." Luisa didn't believe him. After his 'late nights' there was the smell of perfume on his collar. Yet she no longer cared. Carmen was her world now. Caring for her daughter fulfilled Luisa. She dreaded what her life would be like when Carmen grew up and got married.

Carmelita rose at five each morning and knelt on the stone floor. She'd learned to ignore her aching knees and concentrate on prayer.

After ten years in jail, she was now a novice at Convento de San Leandro, a cloistered order having no contact with the outside, Carmelita didn't mind, the world had rarely been a kind or happy place for her. In the convent, no one had ever commented on the way she looked or spoke.

Carmelita liked the routine and certainty her confined existence offered. There was nothing for her beyond the thick exterior walls. Ramon was probably dead and, if not, Carmelita didn't want to be a lifelong burden to him. She missed Beatriz, yet it was best she had come here. Carmelita might have caused trouble for Beatriz if she'd sought her out after being released, and she would have been a burden to her also. After all, who would have employed Carmelita now she had a criminal record?

Although the convent was close to the centre of Seville, inside all was peaceful and conducive to worship. Most days, Carmelita worked in the kitchen, helping to make the yemas de San Leandro. Small, creamy cakes made from a combination of sugar, lemon juice, and egg yolks. When no one else was looking, Carmelita would surreptitiously dip a finger in the mixture and quickly lick it off before anyone noticed. It was the one temptation she couldn't resist.

The nuns followed the same recipe they'd used for hundreds of years. They sold the yemas to the public. A rotating wooden turntable and an absence of windows allowed the nuns to remain unseen.

There were no mirrors inside the convent. "It would encourage the sin of vanity," the Abbess had told her.

When alone, Carmelita frequently ran her fingers over the flesh which now covered what had previously been a gaping hole. Carmelita had recently returned from hospital. The Abbess had bestowed the greatest of gifts upon her by using convent funds to pay for the operation. To Carmelita, it was nothing less than a miracle that she was now blessed to have a normal mouth with only a scar to indicate her past.

Carmelita owned only three possessions: the wooden cross which hung from her neck, rosary beads, and a Bible which she never tired of reading. She was content, she didn't need or want anything more.

CHAPTER 32

At the urging of Brahim, Izil began to attend another mosque in Tetouan, one where the Imam was more radical. Preaching to the faithful at Friday prayers, he was insistent, berating them for their apathy.

"It's several years since the end of the Second World War yet still, my fellow Moroccans, we are living under the colonial yoke of France and Spain. The call for independence from our leader, Sultan Mohammed, falls on the deaf ears of the Europeans. They drove us out of Al-Andalus, claiming it for Christianity, so by what right do they rule us here? Peaceful protests on the streets have been met with bloodshed. It's time, time to rise up with our brothers in Algeria and Tunisia, and in the name of Allah. Time for us to drive out the infidels. It is time for Jihad."

But no mass uprising came and occasional protests achieved nothing. In Izil's cafe in the casbah the men continued to talk about doing something but no one did anything, lethargy had become too deeply rooted. They preferred to leave things to fate, to God's will.

When he stormed into the cafe late one morning in 1954, Brahim's eyes were aflame with outrage.

"Have you heard the news?"

"What news?" asked Izil.

"The French have exiled the Sultan and his family to Madagascar. We must act."

"You've been saying that for as long as I can remember."

"Well, this time I'm serious. We need to do something spectacular which will make everyone sit up and take notice. I have a plan. Remember La Giralda in Seville? I want to blow off the bell tower they stuck on top to remind everyone it was a minaret, and that once we ruled and will do so again. Will you help me?"

Izil was impressed by Brahim's ambition. La Giralda was the tallest building in Seville, visible from throughout the city. Izil thought of how he'd been dragged along the floor and thrown out of La Mezquita in Cordoba and of the other ignominies he had suffered in Spain, disrespected and despised because of his race and religion.

He must decide if he would stand up for his dignity and that of his people or kowtow as he'd done for so many years. There could only be one honourable answer.

"I'd be interested to learn more. Sit down and drink some tea with me."

Carmen bit her lip, hard. It frightened her, her

mother's persistent, hacking cough. It echoed off the walls. She'd been like this for weeks, and today it sounded worse than ever.

When Carmen walked out onto the patio, her mother was almost bent double, one arm against the trunk of an orange tree for support. Luisa quickly scrunched up the white handkerchief hanging from her other hand but Carmen had already noticed the spots of red.

"It's nothing."

"Don't treat me like a child, I'm seventeen. You need to see the doctor."

"Perhaps."

"Perhaps isn't good enough, promise me you'll go."

Luisa sighed. "All right."

Carmen was relieved when her mother told her the doctor had said it was nothing serious and would soon pass. But it didn't, her mother lost weight and her skin became sallow like old paper. Within a short while she took to her bed, telling Carmen she only needed to rest a little.

Carmen joined her during siesta. Cuddling up close, Carmen was shocked how boney Luisa had become.

With her fingertips, Luisa gently stroked her daughter's cheek. It reminded Carmen of when she was a little girl and life seemed endless and untroubled.

"Oh cariño, you've been my greatest gift, my pride and joy. I need you to be brave for me." Carmen immediately felt sick in the pit of her stomach, her instinct had already told her what was coming. "I'm dying. I wish I had longer so I could see you marry and have your own children, but God has decided otherwise so we must accept that. Please don't be sad for long. You have your whole life ahead of you. More than anything, I want you to be happy. Remember, even though you won't be able to see me, I'll be with you at your side, always."

Carmen buried her face in her mother's chest, crying softly.

The funeral was an occasion for the ruling class of Seville to gather in the cathedral. Carmen was grateful for the black veil which masked her emotions. She lifted it only when she bent down to kiss her mother lying in an open casket in front of the altar. The woman's makeup had been expertly applied and her hair perfectly arranged. It was difficult to believe she was gone, difficult to believe her mother would never walk in through the front door, difficult to believe she'd never be able to run into her mother's embrace for comfort when the world hurt.

A solemn face, his features fixed, her father displayed no grief. Carmen knew her parents' love had long ago withered to a mutual dislike and that he had a mistress.

In the following days, Carmen spent a great deal of time in Luisa's bedroom going through her mother's belongings and remembering their times together. Sitting in front of the mirror at the dressing table, Carmen imagined her mother behind her, smiling while Carmen tried on Luisa's jewellery.

Carmen opened the drawers on each side of the dressing table to see what they contained that might spark a memory. Pulling out a neatly folded silk scarf from the bottom drawer, she pressed it against her face, inhaling her mother's perfume of vanilla. She went to put the scarf back to see it had hidden a small blue book.

Curious, Carmen picked it up and began reading. A diary from 1939 when Carmen would have been only two years old. Her interest was pricked, a window into the past, but the contents were mundane. Descriptions of the weather and what was planned for the evening meal, recorded in her mother's small, spidery handwriting.

Carmen soon got bored and leaned down to put the diary back. It slipped from her hand, landing on the floor, open. Carmen's attention was caught by the words revealed, *'a miracle happened today'*. Intrigued, she retrieved it and continued reading:

'God has answered my prayers. Francisco arrived home with the most beautiful little girl one could imagine. She's from the orphanage. Her parents abandoned her. Francisco says her name is Carmen, which is a name I've always loved.

Carmen was distressed. The poor little thing must be so overwhelmed. I am so happy God has sent her to us. Carmen will soon forget the awful start in life she's

had to endure.
I already love her with all my heart.'

Carmen laid the diary down on the dressing table, her heart thumping, her pulse racing, her mind spinning, a Catharine wheel of blinding sparks.

Never once had she suspected her parents weren't her biological ones. After all, they had black hair and brown eyes like her. Yet so did most Spaniards, she scolded herself. Carmen recalled a conversation from years ago.

"Who do I take after, you or Papa?"

"You're a mixture," replied Luisa. "The person you're most like is my mother, who sadly you never got to meet. She died shortly before you were born."

"Do you have a photograph of her?"

"I wish I did. There were some but they were destroyed in a fire at my parents' house."

Carmen had no reason to question what Luisa told her and never thought more about it, not until now.

A need to get out of the house and go somewhere else to think became overwhelming. Carmen ran down the stairs and out onto the street.

CHAPTER 33

"Stop fretting," scolded Brahim while they drove into Seville, swerving frequently to avoid the large potholes. "Everything will be fine. We have it planned down to the last detail, it'll work out perfectly."

Izil rubbed his sweaty palms on his trousers. Yet maybe Brahim was right, getting into Spain had been easy. Arriving in Tarifa on the ferry from Tangier, their bags weren't inspected. Their veterans' cards and an explanation that they'd come to honour their dead comrades and pray at their graves was accepted without question.

Last night, in a backstreet hotel, they put together the bomb after buying missing parts at a hardware shop. This morning, they'd picked up a car from a contact already in Spain. Tonight, a fishing boat would be waiting by a beach near Tarifa, and by tomorrow evening they would be back in Tetouan, mission accomplished.

They came to a halt opposite the main entrance to the old tobacco factory, a gargantuan edifice built in a huge rectangle. A building larger than any in Spain, other than El Escorial, the former royal palace near Madrid. Tobacco, like chocolate, first reached Europe from the Americas through the then port of Seville. Only recently had the former factory become part of the city's university.

When he got out of the car, Izil looked across the street at the building. It was as if the statue of the winged angel on top blowing a long horn knew their intention and was trying to sound the alarm. Izil wished he knew how to drive so Brahim, rather than he, would be the one planting the bomb.

"I'll see you in thirty minutes, Inshallah," said his friend. He drove off, taking safety with him.

Izil made his way along the road and then walked up a side street, wending his way into Plaza de Triunfo and around the back of the cathedral to the foot of La Giralda. It towered above him, topped by el giraldillo, a weather vane in the form of a woman and in the style of a Greek goddess holding a cross. The wind pushed clouds east and La Giralda seemed to move towards him. Izil took a couple of steps backwards to compensate.

For nearly eight centuries La Giralda had dominated the city's skyline. Today, this icon of Seville was about to become famous for another reason.

Izil bought a ticket. "You'll need to be quick, we close in thirty minutes," said the man at the entrance.

Izil began the climb, ascending the stone ramps built wide enough for a horse to enable the muezzin in Islamic times to ride up to make the call to prayer, which had once travelled over the rooftops of Seville five times every single day. Izil passed several people on their way down, cameras hanging from their necks, American tourists, probably. The city was now firmly back on their European tour circuit.

Izil stopped to catch his breath. Approaching forty, he was no longer fit. Hot and dripping with the perspiration of his exertion and anxiety at what he was about to do, he reached the bell tower. Izil had it to himself apart from a young woman with her back to him.

He looked out over the roof of the cathedral and down at the orange trees in its courtyard. Beyond, he could see the rest of the city and the country surrounding it, parched and dun coloured. Above him, hung enormous bells which for hundreds of years had rung out the sound of the infidel.

Izil imagined the explosion. The bells falling, smashed, the very walls of the bell tower collapsing, its masonry crashing through the roof of the cathedral, el giraldillo falling helplessly through the air and breaking into smithereens. What a spectacular event it would be, a victory for the Moroccan independence movement and for Islam.

Izil thought of Beatriz and hoped she was nowhere in the vicinity. After all these years, he still thought of her and their time together. Even though their affair was brief, it was engraved on his memory. Never had he experienced the ecstasy he'd found with her.

Carmen looked down upon the people far below her, small and ant like taking 'el paseo', the evening stroll, a daily ritual, to watch and be watched. She regularly came up here to gaze at the blood orange sunsets of Seville which painted the pain and passion of the city across the sky.

Tonight it would reflect the pain of her own discovery. Were her parents ever going to tell her of her past or had they always intended to keep it a secret? The death of the woman she'd always thought of as her mother had been a huge blow. That she was adopted was yet another hammer, smashing her world into pieces and shattering her sense of self. Carmen no longer knew who she was. Her whole identity destroyed by a few words hidden in a diary never meant to see the light of day.

Izil placed his hands against his jacket pockets, feeling the outline of their contents. He was keen to get on with his task. The girl showed no sign of leaving and Izil could wait no longer. He knew what to do, they'd planned for this eventuality. From an inside pocket, he pulled out a gun.

"Hey, you." Carmen turned towards the abrupt voice, her eyes widening. "Stay right where you are." She froze, a rabbit in headlights.

Taking the bomb from one pocket and the timer from another, his fingers worked quickly, his eyes darting from them to her, ready to grab the gun he'd laid down by his side. Trapped in the far corner from the exit, Izil calculated she wouldn't be able to make a run for it before he could shoot her.

Once all was set, Izil reached into an inside pocket and took out a folded piece of fabric. From his trouser pockets he retrieved stones which he used to hold the flag in place as he placed it on a ledge and let in unfurl so it would be seen by those below. Red, with a green five pointed star in the centre, the seal of Solomon and the flag for an independent Morocco.

Izil cupped his hands around his mouth and yelled out at the top of his lungs, "Allahu Akbar." It thrilled him to think this was the first time in seven hundred years those words had flown out from here. No longer was he afraid, no longer would he turn the other cheek. He and all Morocco, and all Muslims under colonial occupation, would fight for their freedom and win.

Carmen was visibly shaking, not knowing who this mad man was, but knowing her life was in danger. Izil gestured with his pistol, "We're leaving, walk in front of me. Don't try anything stupid and you'll live."

To Carmen, the walk down seemed unending. Twice her legs buckled and she reached out to the walls for support. Salty tears running down her face found their way into her mouth. She prayed to God to spare her, she was too young to die.

When they approached the final ramp, Izil came

closer and placed the end of the gun against the side of her neck. Carmen shuddered at the pressure of steel on her skin. Outside in the sunlight, four civil guards were waiting.

"Stand back," shouted Izil. "If any of you make a move, she dies."

They obliged and Izil backed away towards the waiting car, ensuring at all times his hostage shielded him. The moment they reached the vehicle, he pushed her onto the back seat and joined her. Brahim sped off, nearly ploughing into a man and his donkey sauntering towards them.

Izil regretted they couldn't stay to watch the explosion. He would only get to see the aftermath in a newspaper. Thinking of the adulation he would receive back in his cafe, he forgot his regret and smiled.

Once they were out of the city, Izil put his gun away. For the first time, he observed the young woman in detail. There was something familiar about her, those features. He had seen them before. But where, and who? Then it hit him, she had a striking resemblance to Beatriz.

"Who are your parents?"

"Why do you want to know? So you can seek a ransom?" Her accusation was defiant, haughty even.

Izil didn't pursue the matter. Beatriz had said her daughter had been sent to another part of Spain, it couldn't be her. It must be pure coincidence that they happened to look similar. He returned

to thinking about his triumphant return home. A
hero of the revolution.

CHAPTER 34

Her emotions in tatters, Carmen staggered along a road. In the darkness, a couple of cars passed by, their headlights holding out hope like a lighthouse at sea. They either ignored her or didn't see her desperate waving. She ran after the second vehicle and tripped, falling into a dry ditch. She lost the will to move. Supine, Carmen looked up at the stars, mere pin pricks of light in the blackness entombing her. Exhausted, she fell asleep.

"Are you all right?"A man whose facial features were obscured by the morning sun behind him stood above her.

She sat up awkwardly, stiff from a night on a bed of hard earth and stones. "I was kidnapped and I don't know where I am. Can you please help me?"

An old hand of paper-thin skin reached down. The man led her to his home in a nearby village where his equally wrinkled wife, whose absence of teeth caused her lips to fold inwards, offered Carmen bread and coffee. The hot coffee burned her mouth and the stale bread scratched her throat.

Carmen was utterly miserable but not because of

that or what had happened at La Giralda. It was what she now knew about herself which hurt so much more.

The husband disappeared, returning not long afterwards with the Civil Guard. Before noon, her father arrived. After thanking the couple, he put his arm around Carmen and led her out to his car. While he drove her back to the city he glanced across, noticing the far away look in her eyes. Francisco concluded she must be traumatised from her experience.

"Cariño, you've had a terrible fright. But you're safe now, they can't ever hurt you again. They'll catch the culprits, and fortunately the bomb failed to go off."

Her response was a bomb which exploded his mind. "I found mother's diary. Why did you never tell me I came from an orphanage?"

A sudden outbreak of sweat pricked Francisco's torso. He slammed his foot on the brakes and pulled over. "Because it didn't matter to us where you came from. You've been our daughter since the day I collected you from the orphanage, and our love was as strong as if your mother had given birth to you herself."

"But it matters to me, I don't know who I am anymore."

"You are Carmen Luisa Maria Castillo Morales, that's who you are."

"But my parents-"

"Your mother, God rest her soul, and I, we are your

parents."

Carmen persisted. "I want to know who put me in the orphanage and why."

"You were rescued. They were Republicans, communists. They were caught trying to smuggle you out of the city. They were going to send you to the Soviet Union while they stayed behind to continue fighting and killing innocent people, send you away to a life of horror, abandoned and cut off from your homeland forever."

Carmen buried her face in her hands, shocked at the cruelty of her birth parents. She already knew how awful the Republicans had been. They were monsters who cut babies out of pregnant women, burned churches, and raped nuns. All her generation had been taught these things. In school, she'd learned about Franco's battle to save Spain from a vicious enemy. Few dared ever to contradict that narrative, to do so would get you jailed, maybe made to disappear, no body ever found.

Francisco leaned across and hugged her. "Your mother and I talked of telling you but we decided it would only cause you grief. That's why we kept it from you. Let's get you home."

Over the next few weeks, the thought of Carmen's birth parents consumed her waking hours, burrowing a hollow in her soul. She couldn't stop thinking about what they'd done to her, done to their own flesh and blood.

How could they have been willing to ship her off to

Russia, a godless land where she would have been so alone and afraid with nobody to love her? That anyone could do such a thing to a small child was utterly heartless and unforgivable.

Yet the total disregard they'd shown for her welfare made it easier than it might otherwise have been to consign them to the past and forget about them. They didn't deserve to occupy a place in her mind. Think of them no more, she told herself. They deserve no memory, no acknowledgment of existing. Carmen had no desire to ever meet her birth parents if they still lived.

She accepted Francisco and Luisa hadn't meant to hurt her by keeping from her the truth. She'd been lucky, so lucky to have been saved from parents who didn't want her, and to be taken in by two people who had loved her and given her such a privileged childhood. She was proud to be Carmen Luisa Maria Castillo Morales.

In Tetouan, Brahim rushed breathless into Izil's cafe. "I have wonderful news." The patrons ceased their inconsequential conversations and turned their heads. "France and Spain are giving us our independence!" Cries of 'God is the greatest' echoed around the room and men leapt up and embraced each other.

Two years had passed since the failed attempt to blow the roof off La Giralda but that disappointment no longer mattered. Izil grinned while he thought of arriving home and relaying the happy news to his three young sons. They wouldn't reach manhood under another nation's rule. If they fought, it would be for Morocco and Islam, not for those who for centuries had despised and abused them. They would be free, finally.

Izil thought also of his father who hadn't lived to see this day. He hoped the man was looking down from paradise, proud of his son and of the success Izil had become. The man who as a teenager had walked down from the mountain all those years ago.

Later that day, Izil walked towards the sea and looked out into the deep blue yonder where ocean and sky merged into one. His elation ebbed. Somewhere out there was Spain and Beatriz. He would never get to be with his true love, the woman who had completely captured his heart, and he knew he would die regretting that.

In Seville, Carmen found a happiness greater than she'd ever known. She fell madly in love. Carlos, the son of the mayor, was tall and handsome with an irresistible twinkle in his eyes. It was a whirlwind romance. Flowers arrived at the house almost every day, and when he proposed on bended knee beneath a full moon illuminating the cathedral behind them Carmen didn't hesitate.

Both families approved of the match which was sealed with a grand wedding in the Cathedral.

While her father walked her down the aisle in a wedding dress with such a long train it required three bridesmaids to carry it, Carmen recalled what her mother had said. She imagined Luisa there, next to her, invisible yet present, a guardian angel at her side. When the couple knelt before the priest to pray, Carmen thanked God for her many blessings.

Ramon found it strange to walk through the open prison gates, at liberty to go where he wished. Although only in his forties, the few strands of hair left on his head were grey and he walked slowly and hesitantly, a man unsure of himself, cut adrift in a world he no longer knew.

For twenty years he had laboured at the Valley of the Fallen. The bleak monument was now almost finished, at a terrible cost to the prisoners forced to build it.

Ramon didn't once look back, he didn't need to. That mausoleum glorifying hatred, that place of suffering and gloom, would forever be carved on his mind, memories he couldn't ever escape no matter how far he ran.

Ramon clutched an envelope. It contained a few thousand pesetas, one peseta for each of the days of his incarceration. Money which he'd need to avoid a life on the streets.

In Madrid, he went to a barbers shop to get his beard shaved off. Afterwards, he went into a men's clothing store and bought himself a black suit and two white shirts and a pair of black shoes. Ramon wanted to look his best when he applied for a job. He split the money remaining into two, putting the bank notes into the left and right pockets of his jacket.

From Madrid, he took a train south, travelling third class. His fellow passengers shifted often, uncomfortable on the wooden seats which numbed their backsides and made their spines ache. Ramon didn't notice the discomfort, it was nothing compared to what he'd endured.

Through the window, he could see little had changed for those living in the countryside. On the roads were donkeys not cars, in the fields men not tractors, men who looked as poor as those in his village before the war began.

While the train crossed the empty spaces of central Spain, Ramon pondered on the future which awaited him. He planned to return to Seville in search of work. He also clung to a faint hope that Beatriz might have remained unmarried. First, though, he needed to visit his village.

Sleep overtook him before the train reached Seville. Ramon was woken by the guard to find all the other passengers had already got off.

Walking to the bus station, he patted the pockets of his jacket and abruptly halted. Slipping his hand into the one that no longer had that slight bulge, he almost retched. Half his money had gone, stolen no doubt when he fell asleep. Money which had taken so many backbreaking years to earn.

On the bus ride Ramon forgot his money woes, he faced more important worries to contend with. The moment of truth was fast approaching. Ramon was agitated, anxious with anticipation while he walked out of the village square and down the narrow street to the house, excited to see his mother and sister yet fearful they might not have survived.

Eyes tracked him, the eyes of those seated on doorsteps or leaning against walls, silent in the searing heat and bright sunshine as if outsiders were unwelcome and signalled danger. Those he'd grown up amongst no longer appeared to know who he was.

The old door creaked mournfully on its hinges. Ramon pushed it open. Mice scurried across the dirt floor. Not a single sign of human habitation remained.

When he went back outside an elderly neighbour screwed up his face, seeking to focus. "Ramon, is it you?" Ramon nodded. "I barely recognised you."

"Do you know where my mother and sister are?"

"They took your mother at the start of the war."

Ramon's heart missed a beat, his eyes misted. "Where?"

"Where they took everyone. Come with me." The man beckoned with his hand and waddled down the lane, his legs bowed from a life of poor nutrition.

"And Carmelita?" asked Ramon while he followed.

"They left her alone. Then one day a woman came

to visit her. I remember how glamorous she was, she walked like a queen. They left together, on the bus."

Ramon's spirits rose. The woman must surely have been Beatriz. Carmelita could still be alive.

The man led him down a narrow track out of the village and into a ravine, a place which had once echoed with laughter during his childhood while he played there with friends. A spray of flowers, withered and lifeless lay on the earth.

"The Nationalists shot them and threw their bodies in a mass grave they first made the victims dig. No one was allowed to mourn them or visit. But people did, they sneaked down at night to bring flowers. However, life goes on. Many who remember what happened are now dead themselves or getting old. One day it will all have been forgotten, the terrible things that Franco's men did. I expect you'd like to be left alone," added the man, noticing the anguish on Ramon's face.

Ramon dropped to his knees and wept for his mother. The woman had never harmed a soul, and yet they'd murdered her because they hadn't found him. His mother had sacrificed herself for her son, sent him away so that he would live. What greater love could there be.

Her murderers would have grand funerals and be buried beneath elaborate tombstones, remembered while their victims were forgotten. Ramon hated there was no justice in this life.

When Ramon ascended the hill back to the village,

he could see below the house of Castillo Morales bathed in evening sunshine, a parallel world of wealth and plenty, a world in which the guilty never had to account for their crimes. Another Spain, one for the few, not the many. A Spain which had won the war and kept its boot firmly on the neck of the poor and landless.

Ramon fought the urge to go and confront the man. He wanted to kill him, with his bare hands if need be, make him pay for his crimes. Images of his sister and Beatriz held him back. The living might need him.

CHAPTER 35

In April 1959, on the twentieth anniversary of the so-called 'National Victory', Carmen and Carlos accompanied her father and her husband's parents to the opening of 'el Valle de los Caídos', the Valley of the Fallen. Carmen was blooming, expecting her first child, a child whose future would be secure thanks to being born into a wealthy family.

Alighting from the taxi which had brought them from Madrid, Carmen was immediately struck by the sheer scale of the uncompromising fascist architecture. On top of the rocky outcrop had been constructed the world's largest stone cross. One hundred and fifty metres in height, it was a monolithic confirmation of the power of Franco's regime and that of the Catholic Church over all Spaniards.

At ground level, hewn into the rock face, were archways of cold grey. They entered the vast tunnel-like Basilica to await the arrival of Franco. Thousands were already gathered outside to listen to the mass which would be broadcast over loudspeakers.

Inside the Basilica Carmen heard a tremendous roar of approval, signalling the arrival of El Caudillo. She visualised the sea of arms raised in salute.

The congregation stood in expectation of Franco's entrance. Instead, they heard him speaking to the crowd outside, reminding them of how they'd made the International Brigades 'bite the dust'. He was in no mood for reconciliation and never would be. Franco preached triumphalism.

Ostracised for several years after World War Two, he was now accepted by the West. America had embraced him as a partner in the Cold War.

To make that more palatable, President Eisenhower pressured Franco to promote the Valley of the Fallen as a monument to those who died on both sides of the conflict. Franco paid little more than lip service to the concept. Skeletons of dead Republicans, disinterred without seeking the consent of their relatives, were brought here, but the focus remained as a place of homage to the Nationalists who perished in the civil war.

When Franco entered, he and his wife went to the front and knelt at the altar while high ranking clergy began their rituals. For his supporters, it was an honour to be there. That forced labour had been used and so many were killed during construction was something they didn't care about. Long ago King Ferdinand and Queen Isabella had driven out the Moors, and now Franco had rid Spain of those who threatened the centuries old status quo. Hierarchical and Catholic Spain was once again secure. Carmen and the rest of the congregation kneeled too and gave thanks to almighty God for El Caudillo.

Ramon roamed the streets of Triana, seeking Beatriz. None of those he asked knew her. He thought some probably did but an invisible cloud of suspicion hung over the city. Talking to the wrong person or saying the wrong thing could have you arrested and thrown in jail. La Guardia Civil, armed and standing in pairs on street corners in their sombre grey uniforms and patent leather boots, were a constant reminder of that. 'The crows' quickly dealt with any who strayed beyond the narrow path Franco had imposed on the population.

Ramon found a room to rent across the river in Seville and devoted his time to finding work. His money was fast running out.

Unable to explain what he'd been doing these last two decades, an offer of employment proved elusive so Ramon bought some supplies with the money which remained and set himself up as a shoe shiner. Down on his knees before the city's more affluent inhabitants, he became closely acquainted with their shoes and socks. They rarely deigned to talk to him, and he never initiated a conversation for fear of losing their future custom. While he brushed, Ramon thought about his life and wondered what had happened to

THE SHADOWS OF SEVILLE

that optimistic youth who once thought Seville promised endless summer. The city still seduced with her charm, but those dreams of freedom he'd carried were dead. Franco had strangled Spain's fragile democracy.

Returning for siesta one afternoon, Ramon watched girls in flamenco dresses emerge from a building, giggling. It made him smile but it was a wistful smile. Labouring at the Valley of the Fallen, he'd often daydreamed about how his life could have been, how he might have married Beatriz and had children, maybe a girl who would have become a dancer like her. Yet now he never would have a family. His best years had been spent in prison and that prospect had passed him by.

Ramon halted and watched the girls go down the street hand in hand, a picture of contentment. They were too young to have known the horrors of the war and he was at least glad about that.

Behind him, he heard a door closing and turned to see the dance teacher. Like long ago he was too taken aback to speak and she'd already passed him before he managed to get a word out.

"Beatriz!" She turned and surveyed him quizzically. "It's me. Ramon. I've been searching for you, it's so wonderful to find you again at last."

This time there was no smile. Her acknowledgement was a frown. "I know all about you and what you did. Frankly, I'm surprised you have the cheek to show your face."

Beatriz began walking quickly away. Ramon

hurried after her.

"I don't know what you mean."

"Let me remind you then, or have you forgotten that you fought for the Legion?" She stood arms akimbo, her eyes narrowed, her anger unconcealed, her contempt unmistakeable.

"No, I will never forget that. But I didn't have a choice. I was taken prisoner and told they would execute me or I could fight for them. I escaped at the first opportunity and went to fight for the Republicans." Beatriz's wall of certainty began to crack. "Could we get a coffee and I can explain?"

"Everywhere's shutting up for siesta. We can sit on that bench over there, in the shade of those trees."

Ramon told Beatriz his story, of his capture in Paris, and twenty years at the Valley of the Fallen. While he spoke, the hostility in her eyes was replaced by empathy. Yet there was one thing he failed to mention.

"And your lover, in Toledo, what happened to her?"

"I never had one, only you. Who told you such things?"

Beatriz recounted what Francisco Castillo Morales had said to her.

"That man has always hated me. His family owned our village, he still does. I believe it was him who had my mother murdered. He lied to you. I expect he thought making me out to be a traitor to the Republican cause and unfaithful to you would help him make you his mistress." Ramon changed the subject, eager to find out about his sister. "Is

Carmelita with you? A man in the village said an elegant woman came for her. I knew it could only be you."

"Yes, it was me." Ramon's face brightened, he was going to see his sister again. Beatriz saw that and laid a hand on his. "One day she disappeared, she didn't come back. I tried to find her but never did. I'm sorry, Ramon."

He raised his other hand to wipe his eyes. Once again his hope of a joyful reunion had turned to dust. He had no family. Castillo had robbed him of those who loved him, those he had loved. "Thank you for going to get her. It helps to know she got out of the village and spend time with you."

"I was extremely fond of her. We spent some good times together."

"I'm pleased she got to experience happiness, her life was so hard. If only I could have been there for her and my mother. It fills me with guilt."

"There's no need to feel that way, it wasn't your fault. I can see from your appearance you've suffered."

Ramon decided it was time to confess and tell Beatriz the secreth he'd carried within him for so many years.

"There's something I need to tell you. Before I managed to escape from the Legion, I shot a man, a Republican. We were ordered to attack Badajoz. Those of us who'd been forced to join the Legion were made to go out in front. It was him or me, I chose me. I should have chosen death and honour, not a life of shame." Beatriz said nothing and Ramon went to stand. "I should go."

She put her hand on his arm. "No, wait. War is barbaric, it offers only impossible choices. And why do you assume he would have lived if you had died? Franco's army didn't take prisoners. It's time to let the guilt go."

Ramon saw logic in her argument. Those not killed fighting had been massacred when the Nationalists took the city. Maybe she was right, sacrificing himself wouldn't have made any difference.

Ramon looked at her hand on his arm, a hand he had once kissed, a hand which had once touched him with such exquisite gentleness. It bore no ring.

Ramon seized his chance. "Would you like to have tapas this evening?"

"Not tonight. I'm still dancing if you can believe it."

"Of course I can, you look amazing for your age." And indeed she did, even if crow's feet at the corners of her eyes and a few small wrinkles around her mouth had made a home on her face. Ramon observed that, sadly, there were no lines from laughter and smiles. "Some other night then."

Beatriz let her hand drop. "Let me think about it. It's been so many years, Ramon. I thought I'd lost you. I got used to it. I got over you. The truth is I don't have those kind of feelings for you any longer, and I don't know if I ever will. But I'm so happy to have seen you again and to know you lived and that you're now free."

Ramon fought to conceal his disappointment. He'd always imagined if Beatriz wasn't married, they could take up where they'd left off. "Out of prison, but not free. None of us will be while Franco remains in power."

"That's true, and even when he's gone, freedom, if it comes, won't erase the pain so many must endure each day. Adios, my dear friend." Beatriz planted a quick kiss on his cheek and departed. Ramon remained seated, reeling from their encounter.

That night, Ramon lay awake thinking of his lost family. His mother, not even accorded a proper burial after a life of Catholic devotion. And dear Carmelita, she'd deserved so much more than the life she'd endured. As for Beatriz, Ramon fully expected her to be married so to find she wasn't and yet didn't want to rekindle their love wasn't quite the blow it might otherwise have been.

Beatriz also struggled to sleep. Her life suited her. She was independent, a rare thing for a woman in Spain. Dancing still soothed her soul and took her to a place where there was no pain and no regrets, and teaching others fulfilled her.

Beatriz had buried her memories, but the ghosts of the past had returned. Did Ramon deserve to know he had a daughter?

What was the point of telling him, she reasoned.

It would only add to his sense of loss, another family member who was unreachable, a daughter he would never meet. Before the first hint of dawn lightened her bedroom she'd made her decision. Some things were best left unsaid, some secrets best kept locked away in the heart.

CHAPTER 36

Ramon's customer placed his money in the wooden bowl by the side of the tiled public bench Ramon used for his work and wished him good day. Another pair of feet arrived and Ramon began polishing.

The rustle of paper caused Ramon to look up. The man was reading 'Arriba', the official government newspaper. He turned a page and briefly lowered the broadsheet, revealing his face. Ramon stopped, unable to believe his eyes.

"Get on with it, I'm in a hurry," complained the man from behind his paper.

Ramon put his head back down and continued, his heart beating at double its normal rate. He vigorously rubbed his cloth on the shoes until they shone as brightly as the Sevillian sun, but his mind was a gathering storm of dark clouds, seething and distracted by the person before him. The man had aged but, thanks to an easy life, much less than Ramon.

The man threw coins in the bowl and departed without a word. Men like him didn't thank those who served them. Ramon watched him go, a swagger of self righteousness in his stride. Ramon's nemesis, Francisco Castillo Morales.

He hadn't recognised who Ramon had become, or maybe retained no memory of him at all. To Castillo, Ramon had only ever been an irrelevance, a mere peasant, a bug to be squashed underfoot if he got in the way.

Castillo turned the corner. Ramon got up and hurried after him, still not knowing what he would do when he caught up with him. If Ramon had a knife on him, he would have gladly run it through the man. Wanting to see Carmelita and Beatriz held Ramon back from attacking Castillo in the village but things had changed. Carmelita was missing, almost certainly dead, and Beatriz didn't want him.

The streets were crowded and people ambled along in that relaxed manner Seville's climate demanded. Ramon pushed through the throng, darting this way and that but it was too late, Castillo had disappeared. Ramon wondered if the man lived in the city or whether he was in Seville on business. He needed an answer.

Ramon returned to the dance school and waited until the students left before he went in.

"It's all right, I didn't come to ask you out," he volunteered, observing Beatriz's expression. "I saw Francisco Castillo Morales in the street. Do you know where he lives?"

"Let it go, Ramon. You've only just got your life

back. Try to find happiness, living in the past will only bring you pain. If you do anything, the government will kill you."

"I don't care. All those who committed war crimes are still out there, enjoying a good life as if nothing happened. He should face the consequences for what he did."

"I don't know where he lives and I don't want to know. I too once believed hatred and revenge could make everything better but they don't, they consume you like a cancer. All you succeed in doing is keeping the hurt alive. Don't let the thought of him continue ruining your life. Start looking for love, Ramon, not revenge. Listen, I'm meeting a friend later for coffee. Josefina was widowed last year but she's only my age. Come join us, I think you'd like her."

"I'm not sure."

"Come on, give it a try. You've nothing to lose."

Josefina too had once danced but gave it up when she became a mother. Ramon liked her sense of humour but she didn't make his heart beat faster.

"I hear they're filming a big Hollywood movie at Casa de Pilatos on Saturday. It's about Lawrence of Arabia. Apparently, he was an English war hero who helped the Arabs rise up against the Turks in the First World War. We might get to see some film stars. Did you fancy going to have a look?" Josefina asked Beatriz.

"I can't, I'm teaching. I expect Ramon is free,

though."

Under the expectant stare of both of them, he agreed to go. They arranged to meet at the entrance.

Josefina gave him a slightly uncertain finger wave as he approached. "They're not letting anyone in while they film. Have you been inside before?"

"No."

"You should come back, it's really beautiful. The tiles are incredible, such vibrant colours. I can see why they've chosen this location. It has a definite Arabian feel. In the main courtyard, you could easily imagine you were in Cairo or Damascus."

"Another day then."

"How about we go along here instead," she said, pointing. "There's a convent where the nuns make the best yemas in Seville."

Walking off the street into the convent's courtyard, Josefina led him towards a wooden turntable set in the wall.

"You put your money on it," she explained, "and they spin it around and send you back the yemas. The prices are on that board."

"I take it they must be a closed order. I can't understand why anyone would choose to shut themselves off from the world like that. Let's get a large bag, I'm hungry." Ramon placed the money on the turntable and spun it.

On the other side, Carmelita's stomach somersaulted. It had been so many years yet it sounded exactly like him. She wasn't supposed to speak to those on the other side but how could she let this opportunity go, it would never come again.

"Ramon, is that you?"

"Who are you?"

"Carmelita."

His ears were stunned by what they heard and his jaw dropped open. "It doesn't sound like you."

"I had an operation."

"Can I see you?"

"We aren't allowed visitors. Come to the service this evening, I'll be on the other side of the iron grille. I'll speak to the Abbess and ask for permission to speak to you afterwards. I can't talk anymore." She spun the turntable.

Ramon turned to Josefina. "I need a moment." He ignored the bag of yemas and went over to a bench and sat down, putting his head in his hands.

Josefina picked up the bag and joined Ramon. "That was my sister. I thought she was dead."

"Oh, that's so wonderful."

"Do you mind if I go, I need some time alone."

"No, of course not."

"Keep the yemas, I've lost my appetite."

Ramon went back to the austere room in Macarena he rented and sat down on his narrow bed, a place of loneliness, of nightmares and broken sleep. He didn't hear the loud footsteps of the neighbours above or the shouting of the boys outside kicking a football around. His mind was filled by one thing only. That his sister lived was indeed wonderful, but how bitter sweet that Carmelita should have become a cloistered nun. Ramon wondered what could have made her do such a thing.

He arrived early for the service and sat on the end of the pew nearest to the floor to ceiling grille separating the nuns from the congregation who would sit in the main part of the church and look towards the altar. When the nuns filed in, Ramon searched for Carmelita. He thought her eyes smiled when they briefly caught his, but it was difficult to see her face through the grille. Ramon wasn't religious but he prayed to whatever higher being there might be that his sister would be allowed to talk to him.

At the end of the service, Carmelita stood to leave with the other nuns. Ramon stood too, bereft to watch her go and disappear from his life again without even a word. He wanted to shout out at her to stay, but the solemnity of the location choked off his voice.

Carmelita passed in front of the grille and turned her back on him. She unclenched her fist and pushed a folded piece of paper through the grille. It fell to the ground as soundlessly as an autumn leaf. Quickly, Ramon grabbed it and left the church. He went down a side street where he could be alone. With shaking hands, he read her note.

My dearest Ramon,
I'm so happy to know you're alive. I have prayed every day for it to be so and God has answered my prayers. Doubtless Beatriz will have told you about our dear

mother.

Please tell Beatriz I am so sorry I failed her. Little Ramona was brought to the house where I cleaned on the pretext she was an orphan, the house in Seville of Francisco Castillo Morales. I tried to get Ramona out of there and bring her back to Beatriz, but he caught me as I was leaving with her.

I spent many years in jail, in misery. A nun, who visited me in prison, saved me by advising me to dedicate my life to God. She taught me to read and write and brought me to the convent when I was released. I am truly happy here.

May you and Beatriz both find solace in each other and in the knowledge that your daughter will, I'm sure, have been well cared for and is loved.

God bless you and Beatriz, and Ramona too,
Your loving sister

Ramon read the letter twice to confirm he hadn't misread it. A daughter. He had a daughter. A daughter who'd been stolen. Stolen by that tyrant Castillo.

Ramon spent a restless Sunday pacing the streets like a hungry wolf, impatient for Monday to arrive.

CHAPTER 37

Ramon was outside the dance school first thing, waiting for her to arrive.

"Ramon, what are you doing here?"

"We need to talk, inside." He shut the door behind them, his eyes stern and accusing. "Why didn't you tell me I had a daughter?"

"Who told you?"

"Answer my question first," he demanded.

"I wanted to spare you the hurt. I thought you'd already suffered enough with your mother and sister gone. She was taken from me when she was only two." Tears brimmed in Beatriz's eyes. "She was kidnapped by the fascists, sent to somewhere else in Spain, somewhere I would never find her. For a long time I wanted to kill myself to end the awful heartache. I didn't want you to have to endure that kind of pain too."

Ramon's face crumpled and he broke down. To lose his mother, to have a sister he would never be able to talk to, and now a daughter he'd most likely never get to know was too much to bear. Beatriz moved towards him and they held each other in their grief.

After a while, Ramon pulled away. "You named her after me."

"Yes, Ramona. How do you know these things?"

"Carmelita told me."

"Carmelita?" Beatriz's face brightened. "Where is she? Can I go and see her?"

"She became a nun, in a closed order." Ramon related how he'd made contact and reached inside his pocket. "Read this."

Crestfallen to find out that her daughter had been in Seville all the time, Beatriz's shoulders sagged while she read the letter. "When Carmelita didn't come home, I went to the house where she worked. The woman must have lied to me, she told me she'd fired her."

"We must go there and finally have it out with Castillo. I'll bring a knife and-"

"What will that achieve? Ramona, or whatever they have named her, has spent her life with them. She must love them. She thinks he and his wife are her parents. If you attack him, any chance there might be of establishing a relationship with her will be lost, not to mention you'd probably be executed. No, you will do no such thing," insisted Beatriz, her eyes brooking no dissent. "I'll go and watch the house, there's a cafe on the other side of the street. Even if she no longer lives there Francisco probably does, and at some point she'll visit."

"Can I join you?"

"So long as you control your emotions and let me do the talking."

Before they left, Beatriz pinned a note to the door to say classes were cancelled for the week due to a family matter.

They sat down at a table outside, opposite the large wooden doors which Beatriz had knocked upon so long ago to enquire about Carmelita. The shutters on the windows overlooking the street were closed, a barrier to keep the outside world at bay. Beatriz recalled how Carmelita had told her that only the shutters overlooking the internal courtyard were ever opened. Their privacy was total.

Beatriz sighed. "To think that all these years our daughter was here in Seville, behind that wall. If only I'd known I could have got her back, somehow. I believe I may have seen her once, when she would've been about twelve. I noticed a girl staring at me through the open door at my dance class one day while I was teaching. There was a resemblance. Only moments later I went out onto the street to find her but she'd gone. I told myself I must be imagining things, that there was no way she could be in Seville."

"Tell me, what was she like when she was little?" asked Ramon.

Beatriz smiled as she recalled that precious time. "She was beautiful, mischievous, chuckling all the time. A bundle of joy you just wanted to cuddle and smother with kisses." Beatriz's happy expression vanished like the loss of light when a cloud crosses the sun. "I'm so nervous, Ramon. I've been waiting my entire adult life for this moment but it might all go horribly wrong."

A woman approached the door and rang the bell.

"She looks like the cleaner," commented Ramon.

Whoever opened the door to let her in didn't reveal themselves. A few minutes later the door opened once more and out stepped an elegant young woman in a lime green dress, her black hair swept back off her face and pulled into a bun at the back of her head.

Ramon wondered if Beatriz's mouth had suddenly become as dry as his own. "She's the spitting image of you," he whispered.

Beatriz got up and began following the woman.

When she turned the corner, Beatriz called after her. "Señora!" Beatriz had already spotted the wedding ring on her daughter's finger.

Carmen turned. She was unable to mask her surprise. It was as if she was standing in front of a mirror showing her how she would look in another twenty years.

"Ramona, do you know who I am?"

"My name is Carmen, but yes, I can see we look alike."

Beatriz exhaled, hope expanding inside her.

"And I suppose you're my father?" said Carmen looking at Ramon. He nodded, unable to speak, raw emotion coursing through him. Carmen's nostrils flared and anger coloured her cheeks. "I know what you both did, how you abandoned me and tried to send me to Russia."

"That's not true," began Beatriz.

"I don't want to listen to your lies. You're despicable! You may have given birth to me, but you're not my mother in my eyes and never will be, and nor will he ever be my father. Don't bother me again or I'll report you to the police."

Before her parents could respond, Carmen walked quickly away, her stilletos loud, a sharp reminder not to follow.

They stood in dejected silence, the weight of history heavy on their shoulders. Beatriz spoke first. "It's no good, Ramon. We lost her long ago."

"But she's been lied to."

"All of Spain has been lied to. While Franco lives, the truth will remain buried. I always knew our chances were small. Go live the rest of your life. Find happiness before it's over, and keep in touch. I must go."

Beatriz walked off in the opposite direction so Ramon couldn't see her cry.

CHAPTER 38

Unsettled, the buzz of the city which Carmen loved grated. Her breaths shallow, she needed calm, privacy. Carmen took a side alley and a route home she was confident would avoid them.

Entering the hallway, she could hear shrieks of laughter from the courtyard. Her young daughter, Luisa, playing a game of chase with the nanny. Carmen was in no mood to join them. She took off her high heels and crept up the stairs to her bedroom and sat down on the bed.

Carmen had often thought of what might happen if she ever met her real parents, and how she'd find satisfaction in getting to tell them exactly what she thought of them. Yet the encounter hadn't brought closure, only anguish. She looked down at her slender fingers and tried to steady them but she couldn't stop them trembling.

Carmen wished she'd never found her mother's diary and that this morning had never happened. While her mind bombarded her with conflicting feelings, she bit the flesh at the top of her thumb.

Getting down on the floor, she pulled out a wooden

box from under the bed. Once a bright red, the paint was chipped and faded. She lifted the lid and rifled through childhood mementoes. An old doll with one eye missing, a picture of her in the dress she'd worn for her first communion, and a painting of a black cat she'd done many years ago at school.

Finding what she wanted, she pulled out the small rectangular white card, now yellowing at the edges.

"Learn flamenco with Señorita Beatriz, Seville's leading dancer. Classes every morning, except Sunday."

Carmen turned the card over and over in her hands, thinking. It was the same woman, she was certain of it. She visualised that evening at dinner years ago, asking to go for lessons, the surprise of her father's outburst. Was it really because of the dancing or was it when her mother had mentioned the name Beatriz?

Carmen couldn't remember exactly but her gut told her it was only when the name Beatriz was mentioned that he'd flown into a rage. He rarely got angry in front of his daughter. Indeed, that was probably the last and only time.

From downstairs, came a shout of "Hola!" and screams of delight from her daughter running to greet her papa, home for lunch and siesta. Carmen realised she'd lost track of time. She put the card back in the box and pushed it under the bed.

That afternoon while her husband lay sleeping in the half light, Carmen stared up at the ceiling, fretting.

After a week of loss of appetite and sleepless nights, Carmen decided she must find out. Her past could no longer be hidden in a box under the bed and forgotten.

She waited outside the building, listening to feet echoing off the wooden floor and a record of guitar music and raucous calls. Once the students departed, she entered.

Beatriz was in the corner with her back to her daughter, putting the record back in its sleeve. Carmen coughed to attract her attention.

"Oh, it's you. I-"

"I want to hear your story," demanded Carmen.

"Let's sit down, it's a long one." Beatriz led her daughter to straight backed chairs lined against the wall.

Beatriz explained how she and Ramon met, how the Nationalists killed her father and brother, and how she told Ramon to flee to save himself.

"Then I found out I was pregnant. You brought me so much joy after such sadness. The two years I had with you were the happiest of my life.

"Francisco, the man you've probably always thought was your father, came to one of my shows. He asked about my life and I told him about you and Ramon. He said he might be able to help me find Ramon, and to go to his office which I did. He told me Ramon was fighting for the Legion and had another woman in Toledo. I believed his lies. He...this is difficult to tell you." Beatriz looked down at her hands for a moment before continuing. "He tried to force himself on me and I fought back. As I ran away, he shouted after me and told me I would pay.

"It wasn't so long after that I came home to find you'd been taken. Those who seized you told my mother they were taking the children of so-called traitors to be placed with Franco supporting families in other parts of Spain where their real parents would never be able to find them. I went to all the orphanages in the city to see if you might be there. It was the worst thing that has ever happened to me. For a long time, I wanted my life to end. I lost all hope of ever seeing you again.

"Then, only recently, Ramon returned to Seville after twenty years of imprisonment for having fought for the Republicans. By chance, he came across his sister, Carmelita, who is now a nun. She came to live with me after the war started. You loved her and she loved you.

"Shortly after you were taken from me she disappeared. It turns out that Carmelita worked as a cleaner for Francisco's wife, something I never knew. It seems when she discovered you were at their house, she tried to escape with you and bring you back to me. But Francisco caught her before she could get you away and she was thrown in jail. "Finally, knowing what had happened to you and where you were, I had to try and talk to you."

Gently, Beatriz stroked her daughter's cheeks to remove the tears running down them. "I'm sorry to cause you all this hurt, but I thought you should know who you really are. I'm sure Francisco and his wife have loved you as their own, and I'm glad you're safe and well. I only wanted you to know the truth, to know how much I have always loved you and always will."

Carmen stood up sharply. "I need to go."

"Will I see you again?"

"I don't know."

Beatriz watched her daughter leave, not knowing if she would ever return. It was such a gift to have seen her and to have had the chance to explain. But the pain of being apart from her daughter, a pain which had dulled over the years, had become so much stronger now that they'd met again, reopening a constant restless torment deep within Beatriz.

Her mind in turmoil, Carmen walked down to the timeless Guadalquivir. She sat down on the ground and dangled her feet over the edge while she considered the enormity of what Beatriz had told her.

Carmen believed her mother's account. Her lack of hesitation and the absence of contradictions in her story combined with the honesty in her eyes confirmed she was telling the truth.

It wasn't merely that Francisco hid that she was

adopted. He'd arranged to have her kidnapped as a young child, taken from her mother.

The shock was almost too much to absorb. Her entire life was built on a horrendous lie, and the man she'd adored as a father for all these years had turned out to be immoral, a man without a conscience.

Looking across at the buildings of Triana lining the opposite bank, Carmen tried to imagine how her life should have been.

Maybe she would have become a dancer like her mother. She most certainly wouldn't have been rich. She wouldn't have had her own horse or gone shopping in Paris. But what did that matter? True happiness wasn't to be found in money or possessions. And she would most probably have been freer to express herself, not be so controlled by convention and expectation which had kept her confined to a narrow path of dutiful daughter and wife.

Francisco had become repulsive to her. Yet Carmen was trapped, caged like a songbird.

Her husband, Carlos, was a fanatical Franco supporter. He wouldn't understand how she felt. He would tell her to count her blessings she'd been saved from poverty and immorality.

He might even reject her and throw her out if she told him the truth, horrified he'd married a gitana's daughter and not the daughter of a minor aristocrat like he believed. Then she would probably never get to see her own daughter again, and the new child she had recently discovered she was expecting would be taken away from her at birth. Carmen couldn't take that risk.

Divorce was prohibited and men had complete control over their wives and children. She would have to carry on as if tomorrow was no different than yesterday, despite that today her life had forever changed.

Carmen decided seeing her mother again would only make it harder to bear. She must bury what she now knew deep within her soul and tell no one.

CHAPTER 39

"Are you all right?"

Ramon looked up at his customer. "Yes, fine. Thank you."

Ramon realised he'd probably been grunting. While he worked, his mind saw the face of Castillo in the shoes he polished, mocking him and goading him, working Ramon into a fury he couldn't hide. Not only had the man stolen his daughter but he'd lied to her, painting her parents to be demons so she too would despise them. Ramon couldn't let it go, Castillo plagued his every waking hour.

In a back street in Triana, Ramon found someone who could supply what he needed. Wary of interruption, the man rolled down the blinds and locked his shop door before going to a back room to get it.

It was expensive. Ramon would spend most of what he'd been able to save from being bent double at the feet of others but he didn't care. It was worth it. The blade was serrated. Guaranteed to finish him off, whoever he might be, the man told him.

Ramon went back to the same cafe in Calle de Placentines. The caffeine from drinking three cups of cortado elevated his agitation to new heights. He stood, breathing heavily, almost snorting with pent up rage, ready to cross the narrow street and bang on the huge door opposite. When it opened, he'd throw his entire weight against it, turn his body into a battering ram and force his way into the lair of the beast.

He didn't need to. Castillo emerged, a Panama hat sharpening his sartorial superiority. Ramon followed him. Before long they were in the quiet, secluded streets of Santa Cruz. Ramon looked behind him. There was no one, and not a soul up ahead other than his quarry. The shutters of surrounding houses were closed. It was the perfect spot. No one would see it happen.

Ramon reached inside his jacket for the knife and opened his mouth to call out Castillo's name. He wanted him to turn so Ramon could rush at him and stab him in the heart, and tell him who he was while he did so. Ramon Garcia, son of Elena, and father of Carmen, born Ramona. Castillo would die knowing he hadn't got away with murder and abduction, die knowing that his crimes hadn't gone unavenged.

Two members of la Guardia Civil came around a corner. Recognising Castillo, they saluted him and he stopped to chat. Thwarted, Ramon had no choice but to carry on past them, head down, knife hidden.

Later, calmer and back in his room, he scolded himself. This was madness, he would never get away with it. Beatriz was right. He needed to find a new life, a life worth living, not this joyless existence which offered no future, only hurt and despair.

Seville had become his temptress, his femme fatale. She still smelled of oranges and flaunted her good looks but she would drive him to self destruction if he stayed.

The next morning, Ramon put his spare shirt and a toothbrush in a bag and walked to the station where he bought a ticket for Malaga. He'd heard the fishing villages on the coast were changing fast. Hotels were springing up and vacationers from Northern Europe were arriving in ever increasing numbers for sun and sand. It shouldn't be hard to find work there and start a new life. A place that wouldn't constantly whisper in his ears, torment him that his daughter, his sister, Beatriz even, were all so near but didn't want to see him. Mocking him, telling him he wasn't part of their lives and never would be.

Each morning when she opened the dance school, the filtered sunlight of a new day carried hope. Beatriz wondered if today might be the one. The day when her daughter would come to see her. But time passed, a long time passed, and Carmen never did until hope became so weak she died.

Beatriz imagined her behind those impenetrable

doors in Calle de Placentines, probably with children, children Beatriz would never meet. Yet Beatriz knew she couldn't force herself on her daughter, even if the heartache of not seeing her was cruel and unrelenting, and refused to die like hope had.

Beatriz channelled all her energy into tutoring the girls who came to learn flamenco. She spoiled them with gifts. They were the closest thing to grandchildren she was likely to have.

She tried not to think about the future and when she would become too old to teach. Beatriz didn't want ever to retire, time on her hands, time to contemplate and think about what could have been.

Carmen no longer found pleasure in the things which used to make her happy, social functions, shopping for new clothes, going out for dinner. She mourned for the person she should have been. She'd spent most of her life with her kidnapper, unaware he'd stolen from her the mother and life she was supposed to have.

When Carmen was close to giving birth to her second daughter, she summoned the courage at dinner one evening to tell her husband what she wanted. "If the baby's a girl, I'd like to call her Beatriz. It's such a pretty name."

"Whatever for?" glowered Carlos. "No one in our family has that name. If God sees fit to deny us a son, the child shall be called Isabella after my mother."

He shoved his chair back, scraping the tiles and grating on her nerves. He left the dining room, left her thinking as she so often did these days what she had ever seen in him. The claustrophobia of her marriage made her want to scream, but it was a life sentence. She would never be free to rectify her mistake. There were no second chances for women in Franco's Spain.

After the birth, Carmen fell into a deep void, a well of despair she couldn't see a way out of. She wanted to remain in bed and hide away all day long, to live in the shadows.

"I don't understand you," her husband berated her. "You have everything anyone could possibly want but you mope around the house all day. You need to pull yourself together."

Carmen knew what she needed but she couldn't tell him. It was clearer than ever that his reaction would be the opposite of understanding. Years passed but still she continued to struggle.

A shiver ran down Carmen's spine while she watched her two daughters run across the patio to greet their grandfather. She tried not to wince when he came over and kissed her on both cheeks. Be grateful he now spends most of his time at the hacienda, she reminded herself.

But try as she might, Francisco's presence was like sharp nails scratching her mental wounds red raw again. That evening she found it particularly hard to be in the man's presence and to pretend all was well when it wasn't.

Carlos slurped his gazpacho, drawing a look of irritation from his wife. "What's wrong with you now? You've barely uttered a word all evening."

"I have a terrible headache and the light's hurting my eyes, I need to go and lie down in the dark."

Carlos let out a deep and judgmental sigh.

Carmen's efforts at burying her secret had failed. The angst she felt had only increased these past years. It was grinding her down, and getting through each day remained an effort. She was tearful much of the time and lost her temper with her daughters often, particularly in the days before and during a visit from Francisco.

"What's happened to you, Mama?" Her eldest daughter had asked her only yesterday. "I want our old Mama back."

Carmen realised she couldn't fight it any longer. Checking the dance school was still open, she took her two girls, now nine and seven, along with her. Lessons were finishing for the day and the pupils leaving. Beatriz couldn't hide her delight when the three of them walked. She put her hands together in front of her chin as though giving a prayer of gratitude.

"I'd like to bring Luisa and Isabella for lessons. I haven't told them who you are and I don't intend to," said Carmen while the girls ran around the room chasing each other. "It's complicated. I worry if my husband finds out, he'll disown me. Of itself that wouldn't matter, he has a mistress and our marriage exists in name only. But he could throw me out and keep the girls. You know how Franco's Spain works."

"I understand. This is so wonderful, a gift, an opportunity to spend time with my grandchildren. Thank you." Beatriz reached out and clasped Carmen's hands. "And don't despair. I heard Franco has nominated a successor, Juan Carlos. Things might soon improve. Franco's an old man and he'll die in the next few years. If there's one thing life has taught me, it is things change. Too often it's been for the worse, we're surely due happier times after so many years of hoping and waiting."

"There's something else I wanted to ask you. I'd like to talk with my father."

"I'll write to him."

Carmen moved her head back, surprised. "I assumed you'd be together, after all those years of enforced separation."

"No, he wanted that but I'd moved on. I've been free too long to be beholden to any man and get trapped in a marriage. He went down to Torremolinos at the start of the tourism boom and found work as a waiter. Now he owns a small cafe. I think he's found romance." Beatriz winked at her daughter but Carmen detected a hint of jealously in her mother's forced grin.

When Ramon came, he and Carmen went for a coffee while the girls were having their lesson.

Carmen wanted to know all about his life. She listened intently to his story. He told it with such frankness and fluency she knew he too was telling the truth.

"I've only ever heard one side's version of the war," she said.

"That's because it's the victor who writes history, not the defeated. I live in hope that one day the younger generation will get to hear what really happened."

"I used to be so certain of the righteousness of the Nationalist narrative they fed us at school until I heard things from mother's perspective, and now yours." She paused. "There's something I'd like to do. I want to visit my grandmother's grave. Will you take me?"

Ramon stared into his coffee cup before answering. "It would be too upsetting for you. I went there, there's no grave. Those they killed were thrown in a ravine and covered with earth and rocks. It's such a shame she never got to meet you, she would have adored you."

"I wish I could have known her. Before she died, Luisa told me she would still be there, at my side. Maybe your mother, my grandmother, is also at your side."

Ramon smiled wistfully. "That's a nice thought. Personally, I don't believe in life after death."

"Perhaps you should, it softens the blow of losing loved ones to think we'll meet them again one day."

Carmen hugged him tightly when they parted. For that short moment Ramon's regrets disappeared and he stopped agonising about what he'd lost, all those hugs and kisses he should have had from his little girl, all that joy and laughter instead of so many years of backbreaking toil and misery.

Later that year Carmen got the opportunity she'd been waiting for. She invited Francisco to come and watch his granddaughters perform at the flamenco school show. He was pleased to attend, he didn't say flamenco was for gitanas and loose women, not like he had when Carmen asked to learn.

When they arrived, she led him to a seat on the front row to ensure he would have an uninterrupted view. Beatriz appeared from a side room and Carmen went over and hugged her. Carmen turned her head, pleased to note Francisco's open mouthed shock.

"Remember how you flew into a rage when I wanted to learn," she said when she returned and sat down next to him. Her tone was calm and measured. "Well, now I know why. I know what you did, how you had me kidnapped. I'll keep your terrible secret, but you can't hide what you've done from God. He will hold you to account. And I don't want you to visit us anymore. Oh look, they're about to start." Carmen was enjoying her moment of reckoning.

In that one day the balance of power in their

relationship changed. Carmen never raised the matter again, and Francisco spent his days on his own at the hacienda.

Carmen's daughters became accomplished flamenco dancers and formed a close relationship with Beatriz. The girls didn't particularly like their paternal grandmother, she was too strict and no fun to be with. Instead, they adopted Beatriz as a substitute grandparent.

Ramon came up from the coast every few months to meet with Carmen while the girls had their dancing lesson. He endeared himself to them by always bringing sweets, although they were confused by his presence.

"Who is that man?" asked Luisa, the eldest.

"He's a good friend of Señorita Beatriz, and of mine."

"Oh." The answer satisfied her curiosity and the girl carried on munching.

Ramon was glad he hadn't pursued the desire for revenge he once harboured. Spending time in the company of his daughter and watching his grandchildren grow was infinitely more fulfilling. And, finally, he'd won and Castillo had lost. Castillo might be wealthy but he was alone and unloved, and that, after all was said and done, was surely the worst punishment of all.

CHAPTER 40

In November 1975, some partied until the early hours after a sombre newsreader appeared on television to announce the death of Franco. Others hid away and cried, reminded again of lost loved ones and of a life lived in sorrow. His supporters worried what would happen.

At last, to hope the country could become a democracy and take its rightful place in Europe didn't seem unrealistic. Franco's successor, King Juan Carlos, proved to be an enthusiastic supporter of the idea.

To achieve democracy, compromises had to be made to persuade the old guard to give up the reigns of power. The most significant was 'el Pacto del Olvido', the Pact of Forgetting.

There would be no prosecution of those who had committed atrocities. They would get to live out the rest of their lives in peace and comfort without ever having to face justice. Spain wasn't willing to confront the ghosts of her past who still walked among the living.

When not many months after Franco's death,

Carmen received word Francisco was dying and asking to see her, she took her time to dress for the occasion. Standing in front of her mirror, she smiled with satisfaction.

When she arrived and walked into his room, the eyes of the old man propped up in bed displayed a primordial fear he was about to receive a gitana's curse. The woman before him in a flamenco outfit of flagrant red, large golden hoops dangling from her ears, and a red rose in her hair, looked every bit the image of Beatriz.

"As you can see, I am my mother's daughter."

Part of Carmen regretted what she'd done when she observed how thin and frail he'd become. It made it hard to imagine the cruel man he'd been. Yet old age was no atonement, especially for one who'd lived without apology or remorse for wrong done to others, one who'd faced no consequences for his crimes.

"I've made my last confession," wheezed Francisco, snatching at each breath as if it might be his last. "The priest has pardoned me for taking you, but it's your forgiveness I want. Will you forgive me?" His eyes beseeched her. Carmen wanted to refuse, deny him departure from this world with a clear conscience. "Please, I did it for Luisa. She wanted a child so much."

Carmen considered his dying request while the grandfather clock in the corner of the room remorselessly ticked out the final hours of his life. His reasoning was flawed and duplicitous.

He could have brought Luisa a true orphan, rather than kidnap another's child in revenge for rejection of his unwanted advances. His actions had caused three decades of terrible heartache for her mother and robbed Carmen of her true identity.

Carmen's response was laconic. "I forgive but I don't forget."

At the funeral, Carmen and Carlos exchanged few words. By the graveside they stood far apart. They rarely spoke to each other these days. They lived separate lives in the same house, only coming together for the girls' birthdays and Christmas and when face saving respectability required them to appear together in public.

In 1981 divorce became possible once more and Carmen promptly divorced her husband. She left Seville and her cage in Calle de Placentines and drove to the hacienda, now finally legally hers.

She flung open the shutters, driving out shadow and letting in light. On the sideboard it stared at her, Francisco in in his army uniform heavy with medals. Once she'd admired this photo; her protector, her hero. Now all she saw was his arrogance, his brutality. She flung it in the trash. She dusted the frame containing Luisa's photo, the woman she'd thought to be her mother for so many years and placed it back in position. Luisa wasn't to blame, she'd never known the truth.

The furniture would have to go. It was his, dark,

austere, and it no longer held memories she cherished.

Carmen's daughters came home from university. Carmen was pleased for them. She never got the opportunity to go to one or have a career, trapped by the Francoist dogma that a woman's place was in the home. Carmen sat them down.

"What is it?" asked Luisa. "You look very serious."

"For years I've wanted to tell you where I come from, but I was afraid to because of the risk your father would throw me out and prevent me from seeing you. Now I can finally tell you the truth." Their frowns of concern turned to smiles and hugs of delight when they discovered who their grandmother was.

In Morocco, Izil picked a ripe fig from the tree in his courtyard and sat down on the edge of the fountain. After a busy day at the cafe, it was soothing to absorb the tranquility of this haven with only the blessed sound of life giving water to disturb the peace.

While he ate, he reminisced. Allah had been good to him. Izil may have been born into abject poverty but he'd been fortunate to escape that and live a good life, not having to worry where the next meal would come from.

Izil rubbed his knees, his joints ached from standing most of the day. He was getting too old to run the cafe on his own, and today none of his sons had turned up to help. But he smiled like he always did when he thought of them.

His three sons were his pride and joy. They had all done military service in the Moroccan army, two of them serving in the former Spanish Sahara to the south of Morocco. When Spain left the colony in 1975 Morocco occupied it, contrary to the wishes of the inhabitants. Izil would often remind his sons that now there were only the two Spanish enclaves of Ceuta and Melilla on Morocco's Mediterranean coast to recover to make their country whole.

His introspection was interrupted when his wife appeared. No longer that shy, young woman his mother had picked out for him after he returned from Spain, she possessed a force of character to be reckoned with.

"Read this." She thrust a piece of paper at him. "I blame you for putting such an idea into their heads, always talking to them about Al-Andalus and Jihad and your time in Spain."

Izil read the note, his spirits sinking. The three brothers had left Tetouan, already on their way to Afghanistan to join the Mujahideen and fight the Russians. Two years earlier, the Soviet Union had sent in its army to prop up Afghanistan's communist government.

"I hope you're happy," his wife scolded him, her eyes a storm of pain and fury. She went inside, slamming the door behind her.

Izil's lips trembled while he fought the urge to

weep. He might never see his sons again. His perfect world had been blown apart in a single day.

On a late spring day, Carmen, her daughters, and Beatriz and Ramon, were at the hacienda seated outside around a large oak table chatting. Bees buzzed while they flew from flower to flower, and the effects of paella and a couple of glasses of wine promised a lazy, soporific afternoon.

Beatriz and Ramon each cherished these precious moments, a family life they had for so long been denied. Already in their sixties, they were grateful they got to enjoy happiness when once the future appeared to offer only a loveless bleakness. The abundant sunshine of Spain, once so at odds with their sadness, now matched their mood.

And Spain was that free country Ramon had dreamed of so many years ago in Montmartre, and the government was in talks to join the European Union. An attempted coup by renegade army officers the previous year failed when King Juan Carlos stood firm against it.

"Do you feel like a walk?" asked Carmen. "I have something I'd like to show you."

Beatriz and Ramon walked either side of her, linking arms while they sauntered along a dusty track and relished the warmth of the sun on their backs.

Carmen brought them out of the sunshine and into shadow, to a place of absolute quiet where birdsong was absent, to the harsh brown rock of the ravine and its mass grave. Franco might have been buried by the altar in the Basilica at the Valley of the Fallen, but it was the mass graves all over the country, some marked, many not, that gave witness to the horror Spain had endured.

The top of the grave in the ravine was now covered with fresh soil in which flowers were growing, and behind a large rectangular slab of marble stood guard, words engraved upon it.

"In memory of our loved ones, murdered by Franco's army in 1936. We shall never forget them."

Beneath, in two columns, were the names of those believed to be buried there, including Elena, Ramon's mother.

"I didn't tell you what I was doing because I wanted it to be a surprise."

"Thank you, thank you so much for this." Ramon flung his arms around his daughter. "I'm so proud of you. At last, your grandmother is recognised, and so are the others buried here. No longer are they nameless and forgotten."

"This moment belongs to you both, I'll leave you in peace."

Ramon and Beatriz stood in contemplative silence, each thinking of the past and of their life's journey bringing them to this moment. A journey which had bruised and battered them, remorselessly at times, taking them to the edge of despair and beyond. But in their hearts they knew they were lucky. So many had perished, so many lives snuffed out before they'd barely begun.

Ramon spoke first. "Our daughter's such a wonderful person. Just like her mother," he quickly added.

"You old flatterer," laughed Beatriz. "She's much sweeter than me but I'll accept the compliment. I don't get them anymore. I used to be the centre of attention, eyes fixated on my every move while I danced. Yet I'm much happier now than I ever was back then." Beatriz folded her arms across her chest, it was cool out of the sunshine. "I suppose we ought to go. Don't you have to get back to what's her name in Torremolinos?"

"Alejandra you mean. No, we're no longer together. I can't blame her, I suppose she got tired of always being my second choice. I was planning to spend the night here, and then coming to Seville for a few days. I thought maybe we could go out for that meal we never had."

"And then what?"

"Who knows? You've nothing to fear any longer, you'd always be free to divorce me."

Beatriz playfully punched his arm. "You silly old fool. But yes, I'd like to have dinner with you."

+++
+

AUTHOR'S NOTE

The Spanish Civil War has become something of a footnote in history, overshadowed by the Second

World War which began less than six months after it ended.

Substantial assistance from Nazi Germany and Mussolini's Italy and the use of Moroccan troops gave Franco victory.

He refused to recognise citizens who fled the country as Spanish. When Germany invaded France some were forcibly returned, but many Spaniards who sought refuge in France were sent to Germany to work as slave labour and others to Mauthausen concentration camp in Austria where thousands died.

After the war, Franco commissioned a report on atrocities committed by the Republicans. Learning that his own side had committed atrocities at about three times the rate of his opponents, the report was suppressed, and a false narrative promoted that the Republicans had been the evil ones.

Franco governed with a rod of iron, crushing freedom. He took Spain backwards to a time of complete domination by the Church, and women were treated as the property of men.

Most of the population remained mired in poverty even two decades after the war's end. Finally, Franco relaxed his control of the economy, and that together with the advent of mass tourism to Spain began to see growth and a gradual improvement in living standards.

When I first visited Spain as a young child in the late 1960s, it was visibly a poor and backward country. My memories are of an austere place, of the older women dressed in black, of priests and nuns everywhere, and of Civil Guards in pairs on street corners.

Today Spain is transformed, a prosperous and democratic society with an enviable lifestyle built around family and friends, good food and wine, and a zest for life. Unlike Germany, however, Spain has never truly confronted the horrors of its past Those who committed war crimes were never held to account, and now with the passage of time they never can be. Across the country, there remain many mass graves of unidentified victims.

Franco's policy of taking thousands of children away from their Republican parents still causes heartache. Now elderly, most of those seized from their families will never know who their mothers and fathers were, and the ones who find out will never get to meet their real parents because they are dead.

For me, Seville is Spain's most incredible city. If you haven't been, I whole heartedly recommend it. The architecture is stunning, its history is fascinating, and there are many excellent bars and restaurants. If you are unable to visit, I hope this novel took you there.

This book is dedicated to my fabulous wife, who is not only endlessly supportive of my writing but also creates the most fantastic book covers for me, and to my three wonderful daughters of whom I'm incredibly proud.

ALSO BY DAVID CANFORD

Puppets of Prague

Can the dream of freedom overcome fear and oppression? Friendships are tested to the limit in this saga spanning Prague's tumultuous 20th century. In the summer of 1914 young love beckons and the future seems bright for three close friends, but momentous events throw into stark relief the differences between them that had never mattered before.

Betrayal in Venice

Sent to Venice on a secret mission against the Nazis, a soldier finds his life unexpectedly altered when he saves a young woman at the end of World War Two. Discovering the truth many years later, Glen Butler's reaction to it betrays the one he loves most.

Going Big or Small

British humour collides with European culture in this tale of 'it's never too late'. Retiree, Frank, gets more adventure than he bargained for when he sets off across 1980s Europe hoping to shake up his mundane life. Falling in love with a woman and Italy has unexpected consequences.

A Good Nazi? The Lies We Keep

Growing up in 1930s Germany two boys, one

Catholic and one Jewish, become close friends. After Hitler seizes power, their lives are changed forever. When World War 2 comes, will they help each other, or will secrets from their teenage years make them enemies?

Kurt's War - The Boy who knew too much

Kurt is an English evacuee with a difference. His father is a Nazi. As Kurt grows into an adult and is forced to pretend that he is someone he isn't for his own protection, will he survive in the hostile world in which he must live? And with his enemies closing in, will even the woman he loves believe who he really is?

The Throwback - The Girl who wasn't wanted

A baby's birth on a South Carolina plantation threatens to cause a scandal, but the funeral of mother and child seems to ensure that the truth will never be known. A family saga of hatred, revenge, forbidden love, overcoming hardship and helping others.

Sweet Bitter Freedom

The sequel to the Throwback. Though the Civil War has now ended, Mosa is confronted by new challenges and old adversaries who are determined to try and take what she has. While some hope to build a new South, the old South refuses to die. Will Mosa lose everything or find a way through?

A Heart Left Behind

New Yorker, Orla, finds herself trapped in a web of secret love, blackmail and espionage in the build up to WW2. Moving to Berlin and hoping to escape her past, she is forced to undertake a task that will cost not only her own life but also that of her son if she fails.

Bound Bayou

A young teacher from England achieves a dream when he gets the chance to work for a year in the United States, but 1950s Mississippi is not the America he has seen on the movie screens at home. When his independent spirit collides with the rules of life in the Deep South, he sets off a chain of events he can't control.

Sea Snakes and Cannibals

A travelogue of visits to islands around the world, including remote Fijian islands, Corsica, islands in the Sea of Cortez, Mexico, and the Greek islands.

When the Water Runs Out

Will water shortage result in the USA invading Canada? One person can stop a war if he isn't killed first but is he a hero or a traitor? When two very different worlds collide, the outcome is on a knife-edge.

2045 The Last Resort

In 2045 those who lost their jobs to robots are taken care of in resorts where life is an endless vacation. For those still in work, the American dream has never been better. But is all quite as perfect as it seems?

THANK YOU

I hope you enjoyed reading 'The Shadows of Seville'. I would appreciate it if you could spare a few moments to post a review on Amazon. It only need be a few words.

Thanks so much,

David Canford

ABOUT THE AUTHOR

Writing historical fiction, David Canford is able to combine his love of history and travel in novels that take readers on a rollercoaster journey through time and place with characters who face struggle and hardship but where resilience, love and forgiveness can overcome hatred and oppression.

He has also written two novels about the future, and a travelogue.

David has three grown up daughters and lives on the south coast of England with his wife and their dog.

You can contact him via his Facebook page or at David.Canford@hotmail.com

Printed in Dunstable, United Kingdom